THE
MONTAUK
STEPS

THE
MONTAUK
STEPS

•

Diane Sawyer

AVALON BOOKS
NEW YORK

PRINTED IN THE UNITED STATES OF AMERICA
ON ACID-FREE PAPER
BY HADDON CRAFTSMEN, BLOOMSBURG, PENNSYLVANIA

To my husband Robert, for his love and understanding

To Kirk and Linda Sawyer, and to Barrie and Luis Buenaventura, for their encouragement, love and enthusiasm.

To Colin Sawyer, for his wisdom about the big, wide world around him.

To Grace Murdock and Peggy Nolan, gracious and talented St. Petersburg writers and exceptional friends, for their advice and continued interest in my work.

To Marjorie Jackson, a writer and dear friend from California, for her helpful comments and counsel.

To Charlotte Andersen, for her practical wisdom and guidance.

To those family members and friends who encouraged me.

And last, but not least, to Erin Cartwright, Senior Editor at Avalon Books, for her insightful suggestions, which clarified the story and made it more suspenseful.

Chapter One

Arrival

With the tires of her black Bronco squealing above the triumphal blast of Beethoven's "Fifth," Lilli Masters turned off Soundshore Road onto Main Street. She slowed, and then, surrendering to the clogged traffic, came to a standstill. So this is Grayrocks, she thought, squinting into the bright morning sunshine at a street of quaint shops and a vista to the bay. There were cars, vans, bikes, boat trailers, and people everywhere. She had no idea that Labor Day weekend was such a big deal in Grayrocks.

Out on the bay, a double-decker sightseeing boat tooted its horn and chugged past a bevy of jet skiers wearing psychedelic helmets and wet suits. Sailboats and rowboats competed for space with fishing boats heading for open waters. The waves were crowded with vehicles and people, just like the streets. It seemed to Lilli that everyone in Grayrocks got up early to celebrate the holiday.

She watched the tourists strolling along the jammed

1

streets, peering in the windows of fudge stores, beachwear boutiques, and antique shops. They wore tee shirts and shorts, mainly blue and white punctuated with bursts of red and yellow.

Lilli smoothed her cut-off jeans and white tank top, as she idled her Bronco, content that she qualified as a typical tourist. As a freelance photojournalist, she wanted to blend in, to catch people in the act of being themselves.

First rule in her profession: Posed photos do not sell.

Lilli whipped out her tape recorder. "Perfect," she began, her throaty voice sparked with enthusiasm. "Grayrocks on Saturday of Labor Day weekend is just perfect! Here I am, on the eastern tip of Long Island, gearing up for a whirlwind of activity. There are banners strung across the street proclaiming a sandcastle competition and fish fry at the Wharf. Boat races and fireworks too. I couldn't have picked a better holiday weekend."

She inched her Bronco forward. "Photo ops everywhere on land and sea," she added and made a mental note to check her film supply. She clicked off and tucked the tape recorder into her lucky denim tote. The frayed bag bulged with cameras, lenses, notebooks, and her brand-new field glasses. It had gone on every assignment since she'd begun her career five years ago. Now, she didn't dare replace it and chance spoiling her luck with this big break, doing the "Before and After" series for *Viewpoint* magazine.

Second rule: Don't ever mess with success.

At the stop sign, Lilli peered into the rearview mirror. Her green eyes glistened with anticipation. She tried running her fingers through her windblown mane of red curls. Hopeless, she decided. The humidity was turning her corkscrew curls into frizz. She leaned closer. A sprinkling of freckles dotted the bridge of her nose. Her pale skin had gone beyond rosy, approaching bright red. A stronger sunscreen joined her growing wish-list of necessities.

Lilli turned at the next corner and followed the signs to Baywatch Inn. A pre-dawn rain shower had left shining droplets clinging to peaked roofs, bi-fold shutters, and porch railings of the rambling inns that lined the shady street. NO VACANCY signs sprouted like weeds. Thank goodness she had a reservation.

Some last minute e-mail advice from her best friend, Sue, kicked in. "Lilli, call the locals 'Grayrockers,' 'North Shore folks,' or 'Long Islanders.' But if you value your life, never call them 'New Yorkers.' To them, New York means the city, not the state. They have a love–hate relationship with Big Apple visitors. They love their tourist dollars, but hate their pushy ways."

There it was! Baywatch Inn snuggled behind trimmed hedges, a mere stone's throw from the bait shacks and rowboat-rental huts fronting Grayrocks Bay. The cheerful yellow clapboards would photograph well, set off by the inns on either side. They stood as somber as pallbearers next to the bright canary.

Lilli pulled into the ten-minute parking zone and hopped out of her Bronco. A shell path bordered with marigolds and zinnias led to a screened door that slapped shut behind her. It caught the backs of her slim calves, propelling her headlong into the crowd of young families juggling picnic baskets, floats, sand chairs, pails, and shovels. They seemed hardly to notice her amid the chaos.

Stepping past a blond pre-schooler in a bathing suit sporting goggles on her forehead and a boy toting a fishing pole, Lilli strode to the counter. "I have a reservation. Masters. Lilli Masters. Today, Saturday, through Wednesday," she said quickly, eager to check in and begin working.

The woman behind the counter flipped her thick gray-flecked braid over her shoulder. "Masters . . . Masters," she looked through her reservation book. "Sorry. No Masters listed and we're filled up, all twenty-four rooms. The whole town is booked solid for the holiday. It's Labor Day weekend, you know."

"I made the reservation weeks ago," Lilli said sharply. "Please take another look."

"Don't fret. We'll straighten this out." The woman thumbed through several pages of reservation entries. "It's been a madhouse around here. Somehow I must have deleted your name . . . or never recorded it . . . or put it in my miscellaneous file." She flustered, talking to herself, searching through a stack of envelopes.

"Miss . . . Miss . . ."

"Call me Gram," she said. "Everyone does. It's short for Gram Jenkins."

"Gram, please help me. This is a once in a lifetime opportunity for me. I'm a photographer. I'm planning to shoot Grayrocks over the next few days, capturing the Labor Day festivities before the tourists leave. And then again, after they're gone. I have a magazine interested in—"

"In my little town of Grayrocks?"

"Yes," Lilli said. "My photos will bring business to Grayrocks. I'm sure of it."

Gram smiled. "Would you include pictures of Baywatch Inn?"

"Of course!" Lilli exclaimed. "And some complimentary words too. Especially if you find my reservation slip in there somewhere."

"Sorry about the mess up. We'll find you a place to stay. Tell you what. I have a room that's sort of taken, but it might free up. A woman and her teenage daughter checked in yesterday, but they went out last night and never came back. Could be they ran into someone they know and maybe plan on staying with them. We'll just have to see how the flounder flips." She lowered her voice. "They're from New York City, so good manners aren't their first priority. Uh, you're not a New Yorker, are you?"

Lilli chewed her lip. "No, ma'am. I live north of the city, in Suffern. Of course, I travel into the city for my work. I have no choice, not if I want to eat." She didn't admit that she was born in Brooklyn, often visited her parents who still lived there, and graduated from Fordham University in the Bronx.

Gram peered at Lilli from head to toe. "You could use some meat on those bones. Tell you what. You can stay in my granddaughter's old room until we get the scoop on that woman and her daughter's plans. And I'll try to fatten you up."

"I don't want to impose—"

"Nonsense," Gram said. "It's the least I can do, getting your reservation mixed up and all. Anyway, my grand-daughter, Annie, got married and moved to a home of her own on Surfside Road. Her room's sitting there empty." She took a set of towels from the cabinet behind her and handed them to Lilli. "Here, you can be family."

"I really appreciate this." Lilli took the towels and breathed in the scent of lavender.

"Follow me," Gram said and ushered Lilli toward the stairs. She pointed overhead at the clothesline strung with amusing tourist towels. "A great gift for the folks back home. They're from Patty and Steve's shop, on Bay Street. A really nice young couple, just starting out."

Gram turned left at the top of the stairs. "First we'll take a peek at the room you may be taking over. We're not snooping, mind you. I just want you to see the photograph of Mrs. Betty Morgan and her daughter, Clarissa, on the bureau. You might spot them as you wander around town. I'll warn you, though, you'd be looking for a needle in a haystack. Our year-round population of three thousand swells to nine thousand in the summer and this last weekend of the season is always a muddle. But if you see them, ask them to come and straighten things out. Here we are. Room 204."

Gram turned the passkey in the door. "Take a quick peek." She pointed to the photograph in the chipped frame.

As a photographer, Lilli thought the quality was poor and the lighting harsh. "A strong family resemblance," she commented, noting the prominent nose that overtook each small heart-shaped face. It was obvious from the dark roots both Betty and Clarissa Morgan bleached their hair.

"Now we'll head over to my private quarters," Gram said backtracking toward the lobby. "Here," she handed Lilli a key. "Take this extra key to 204. I have a feeling you'll be moving in there very shortly."

The granddaughter's room took Lilli's breath away. Large colorful oil paintings filled the walls, showing daily scenes of Indian life. "My granddaughter's an artist. That's why I'm letting you borrow her room. Your enthusiasm for your work reminded me of her. I hope you'll be as successful as she is. She has shows up and down the eastern seaboard."

Gram straightened a painting that depicted a warrior in his canoe who braved the churning waves to spear fish. "Critics say she's tapped into the Montauk mystique. Truth is, Annie understands the heart and soul of the

Montauk people. Her husband, Matt, is of Montauk descent."

Gram fluffed the bed pillows. "Well, enough about my Annie. Park out back in a guest space, bring in your things, and make yourself at home."

Gram turned as if to leave and then thought better of it. "I have an uneasy feeling about the Morgans. The mother mentioned they were here to forget about a tragic accident. It seems Clarissa's older sister, Gail, was run over by a subway train and killed, during a drug bust that went bad. Hard to believe that could happen to an innocent bystander. They came here to escape the city for a few days before Clarissa begins her senior year in high school. Between you and me, I think they scraped together hard-earned savings for this vacation."

Gram clapped her hand over her mouth. "I'll say no more. You'll think I'm a busy-body and mention it in your story."

"Nonsense!" Lilli realized that Gram enjoyed chatting with guests, getting to know their stories and reasons for coming to Grayrocks. "You're a keen observer and you're sharing that with me."

"From a photographer, that's a compliment. My daughter, Caitlin, was a photographer. Well, that's another story." Gram plunked down on the edge of the bed. "As for the Morgan women, the heels of their shoes were worn down. And they wolfed down the meal I offered. Those are tell-tale signs of money problems, don't you agree?"

"Absolutely." Lilli liked Gram Jenkins. She had made a lucky choice, picking Baywatch Inn from a list simply because of its claim of 'down-home charm.' She wondered if the Morgans had chosen the inn for the same reason or because it was modestly priced. Judging from the suitcases and clothes that Lilli noticed in the Morgans' room, she agreed with Gram. They could scarcely afford a vacation. "Is their car out back?" she asked.

"No. They came to Grayrocks by train and took a taxi from the station." Gram frowned. "You know how it is, Lilli. Tragedies come in threes. I hope nothing unpleasant has happened to the Morgans."

"I'll keep an eye out for them," Lilli said reassuringly. "Where do you suggest I go first for the most interesting photos?"

"The marina," Gram said with a twinkle in her eye. "It's just around the corner and down a few streets. The guys out there really know how to welcome tourists."

Twenty minutes later, Lilli was snapping photos at the marina. The light was perfect, the water sparkling, the boats bobbing in the gentle breeze. She scanned the faces of the tourists milling around, but she didn't see Betty or Clarissa Morgan.

"What do you think of the tourists?" Lilli asked a dock-worker, who was stirring a can of white paint.

He winked mischievously. "Too bad they can't just send us their money and stay home."

"Seriously," she said, "what's your opinion?"

"They're okay when they stay out of our way, but they like to come to the docks and watch us work. They talk our ears off and slow us down. We treat them to the same baptism rites we each had on our first day here."

Lilli's eyebrows rose. "Baptism rites?"

"You know," he chuckled. "They step in a coil of rope, we give a little tug. They lean close to the edge, we yell 'Timber!' Splash! They take a dip."

Lilli looked over the edge. She could swim, but the water was choppy and the dock pilings were coated with nasty-looking barnacles.

"Don't worry," he said. "The water's not deep and we

keep life preservers on hand. It's all in good fun. Anyway, we're choosy. A pretty young thing comes this way and 'Splash'!" He laughed. "It's better than a wet tee shirt contest at Fred's Fish House."

The way he looked at her when he said 'pretty young thing' was downright cruel. He meant she was over the hill—at twenty-seven. Apparently she was too old and not attractive enough for these guys and their games. Fuming and annoyed at herself for caring, she stooped down to take a picture of a child's gaily-painted bait bucket. The toe of her sandal slipped between two planks and caught. She stumbled and her camera flew out of her hands as she plunged into the water. Like a rock, she sunk beneath the surface and touched down in soft sand.

She pushed off the bottom and flailed her way to the surface. Water spurted from her mouth. Seaweed dripped from her arms. "Help!" she sputtered.

"Come up the ladder!" the worker called down to her. "It's right there in front of you!"

Lilli looked up and saw the smiling faces of a half-dozen dockworkers. Two strokes and she reached the ladder. "My camera. Did anyone see my camera?" she asked. She climbed onto the dock feeling embarrassed. Had she been set up or had she tripped over her own two feet?

"I caught it," said a lanky man, stepping out of the crowd and holding her camera out to her. "I was hoping you'd come back to claim it." His broad smile and rugged looks dazzled her. She twisted the bottom of her tee shirt, pulling it away from her waist, wringing out the water. She wished she didn't look like a drowned rat, but what could she do? On the positive side, her hair was no longer frizzy.

Rule number three, the last and most important rule, buzzed in her ears: Never mix business with pleasure.

Well, some rules were made to be broken.

"Thanks," she said, stepping away from the puddle at her feet. "I'd like to show my appreciation. May I buy you a soda or something to eat?"

"Sure. A soda would be fine. I hear there's a place near here that the tourists don't know about." He extended his broad hand. "Zack Faraday," he said, shaking her hand firmly. She noticed that he didn't wear a wedding ring. This was truly turning into a great day.

"I'm Lilli Masters." She gathered up her bag and dropped the camera in it.

"Judging from all those cameras, I'd say you're a professional photographer."

"You're right," she said.

He smiled again. "And from that Swiss Army knife hanging on your bag, I can tell you're prepared for any emergency—at least on dry land."

Lilli laughed and wiggled the chain that attached the knife to the strap of her tote bag. "A present from my brother, Pete, when I graduated college. He thought I might need it some day."

"To fend off unwanted advances?"

"You know the saying, when life throws you lemons, make lemonade. Pete said, 'when you get in a jam . . .' " She flicked open the knife blade. 'Spread it on bread.' " She had a nervous habit of babbling that hit whenever she met an appealing guy. A nervous habit that sent appealing guys running in the opposite direction—fast.

Zack removed his sunglasses and Lilli looked into his gorgeous gray-blue eyes. "Let's go find that soda," she said.

"Wouldn't you rather change first?" he asked. "We can stop off at Baywatch Inn on our way."

"How do you know where I'm staying? Are you a detective?"

He laughed. "Yeah." He leaned close and whispered, "From New York City." He patted the Baywatch Inn brochure sticking out of her bag. "But my detective skills weren't required. The brochure was a dead give-away."

Chapter Two

Harrison Ford Mania

When the screen door slammed at Baywatch Inn, Gram Jenkins looked up from the brochures scattered across the reception counter. "Well, Lilli," she said, stacking a handful. "I see you're a fast learner. Why waste time changing into a bathing suit? Feel like a dip, jump right in! That's the Grayrocks way."

Lilli laughed. "I think I was set up, Gram, but meet Zack Faraday."

Gram shot Lilli one of those woman-to-woman looks that said, "Go, girl! You caught him, now reel him in."

Gram peered over her glasses at Zack. "What brings you to Grayrocks?"

"A wedding. My cousin Tim is getting married tomorrow to—"

"To Margie Schyler at St. Anne's. The announcement's in the *Grayrocks Gazette*." Gram leaned forward, resting her tanned arms on the counter. "Of course, it was no surprise to me. Margie told me everything, long before she got the ring."

Gram looked left and right, then turned to Zack. "You can't fool me with the sunglasses and phony name. I've seen all your movies. *Raiders of the Lost Ark* was your best. Never losing your hat . . ." she chuckled. "That was really something."

"I'm not—"

"Of course you are. You're Harrison Ford."

"No, ma'am." He raked his fingers through his trendy brush cut. "Zack Faraday at your service, and I don't know beans about acting." He looked at Lilli and shrugged.

Lilli could see the resemblance, too. The crooked smile. The weathered good looks. The same boyish charm. "I'll change into dry clothes and be right back. Then we'll find a restaurant and that cold drink."

"No need to go elsewhere," Gram said. "Step out to my patio. Didn't you read my brochure?" She waved one under their noses. "I provide lemonade and iced tea out there all day long. Come on, Zack. By the way, where's that slouch-brimmed hat of yours? And don't tell me you left it in the jungle. I wasn't . . . born yesterday."

Zack laughed. "*Born Yesterday*. That was a great movie. William Holden, right?"

"Just testing!" Gram pushed her wire-rimmed glasses onto the bridge of her nose. "I wanted to see if you studied the golden oldies. But of course you do. You played Holden's role in *Sabrina*, right?"

Zack threw up his hands and winked at Lilli. "Whatever you say, Gram." He leaned close. "Don't spread the word that I'm in town. I'm scouting a location for my next movie. Too much publicity could blow the deal. Grayrocks is definitely on my A-list."

"A sequel to *Clear and Present Danger?*"

"Could be," Zack said and flashed his dazzling smile.

As Lilli headed toward the stairs, Gram followed. "Don't think I'm trying to steal your man," Gram whispered. "I'm just having fun. Pretending Zack is Harrison Ford breaks the monotony of 'Hello, how are you, have a nice day.' And Zack's enjoying the fuss."

"You had me worried," Lilli said. "I thought—"

"My mind's as sharp as a bait hook," Gram said. "Snappy give-and-take with an intelligent man like Zack, that's my secret. I'll go keep him company while you change."

When Lilli returned, she found Zack and Gram sitting together beneath a floppy yellow umbrella. Zack was sipping a frosty mug of iced tea while Gram showed him the photo of Betty and Clarissa Morgan.

"They haven't shown up yet," Gram was saying. "Mr. Morgan, the husband, just called from New York City. He had expected to hear from them last night. If they don't call by this afternoon, he's closing up his dry cleaning shop and driving out here."

Lilli scooped ice cubes into a mug and poured the sparkling tea to the rim. "You sound concerned, Gram," she said and sat down across from Zack.

"You mean concerned about collecting my money?" She chuckled. "Yes, but their being gone overnight worries me too."

"Do you think something happened to them?"

Gram frowned. "I doubt it. What could happen in little old Grayrocks, but I'm showing Zack their photo anyway. One more pair of eyes looking for them can't hurt." Gram squeezed another lemon into her tea. "Mr. Morgan was real snippy on the phone. I mentioned that his wife was all smiles when she left here Friday night. He accused me of hinting that she had a roving eye."

Gram huffed. "When I asked if he wanted me to mention their disappearance to the police, he sassed me. 'Mind your own business,' he said. Well, quite frankly, I pride myself on keeping my nose where it belongs. What crust!"

"He's upset, so he took it out on you," Zack said. He patted Gram's hand and Lilli saw Gram melt under Zack's gaze.

"Where did they say they were going?" Zack asked.

"They didn't say."

"Just out of curiosity, do you remember what they were wearing?"

"White slacks, both of them," Gram said. "The daughter had a blue and white striped tee shirt."

"And the mother?"

"A red, clingy top. Scoop neck. The sexy type that men like. And, for the record, I didn't mention that to Mr. Morgan."

Lilli ran her fingertips along the collar of her white cotton shirt. Plain-Jane white shirt and white shorts. What had she been thinking? She looked like she was on her way to a tennis match, not on a date.

Gram said, "I'd better put this photo back in their room, in case they turn up soon. After all, this is Grayrocks, friendly and safe, not like your big cities."

"Hold it right there!" Zack threw up his hands defensively. "I remember reading about some skullduggery on an island near Grayrocks. As I recall, it happened during an archeological expedition."

Gram flustered. "Great recall, Harrison. I nearly forgot about your detective skills in *Witness*. You're so right. There was some trouble. My granddaughter, Annie, and her husband, Matt Revington—though they weren't yet married then." Gram closed her eyes and sighed. "What a gorgeous couple. She's an artist. He's a consulting archeologist and owns the Grayrocks Marina. Now where was I? Oh yes, a member of the archeological team on Big Shell Island threatened their lives. There were some tense moments—I won't deny that—but it all worked out. My daughter and son-in-law, Annie's parents, weren't so lucky."

Gram's eyes glazed over and she dabbed at the corners with a tissue. "They were murdered. By greedy people who wanted to grab Big Shell Island's prime land."

"I'm sorry," Zack said. "I didn't mean to pull up such painful memories. But it proves that crime can occur in small towns as well as big cities."

Gram pursed her lips. "But it's a matter of degree. Cities attract crime, the way light bulbs pull in moths." She folded her hands and plunked them down on the table. "I'll admit small town folks can be too trusting. We forget that city people often come here with evil in their hearts. So I'll keep on the alert for any trace of the Morgan women."

Zack stood up. "Good idea. And I'll work on my role of the big-city cynical detective, expecting foul play around every corner. Do you know anyone who has a scanner? I'll make a few copies of the photo and show them around."

"My office is filled with cutting-edge high-tech equipment," Gram said, jumping to her feet. "We may look quaint around here, but we're living in the twenty-first century, just like city folks. This is so exciting. Follow me."

Lilli picked up her tote bag. "Have fun, you two. I'm

off to the fishing pier to take advantage of the crowds and the sunlight."

"I'm headed that way," Zack said. "Mind if I tag along? Just give me a minute to run off some copies."

Zack winked at Gram as he scanned the photo. "Maybe Lilli's on this case, too. Photographic skills are essential to police work."

"Then get cracking," Gram said, shooing both of them toward the door. "Time's a-wasting."

Lilli and Zack ambled down the street toward the row of bait shacks. They laughed about Gram's vivid imagination and her love of movies.

"That's the kind of scene I'm interested in," Lilli said. Children were gathered around Salty Jack's bait shack. Kneeling down, she began snapping pictures.

A boy with his cap turned backward screwed up his face and said "Yuck," as he picked through a selection of fat worms. "Wonderful," Lilli said. Snap! Snap!

The boy's friend with sunburned shoulders said "Gross," as he chose oozy fish guts. Snap!

The freckle-faced girl said "Eeuuu," as Salty Jack scooped up their slimy purchases, flung them onto a scale, then dumped them into plastic bags. Snap! Snap! Snap!

The parents, reeling back from the smell, waved some dollar bills toward Salty Jack. Snap!

"Tie them bags tight, kids," Jack said. "Don't let the worms wriggle their way inside your shirts." He chuckled. Snap! Snap! "I hate to see good bait go to waste." He pointed at his belt. "That's waist, W-A-I-S-T," he spelled out the word and laughed heartily at his own joke.

Lilli thanked Jack, the kids, and the parents and tucked her camera back in her tote bag. Zack had been working his way from one bait shop to the next as he waited for her. "No luck," he said. "No one here has seen the women."

"The Morgans are on vacation," Lilli said. "And probably not interested in sticking to a time schedule. Maybe they picked up some cute guys and partied all night."

Zack cocked his head to one side. "Is that what you do when you're alone in an unfamiliar town?"

"Yeah." Don't I wish, she thought, but she said, "Cute guys are in real short supply these days."

At the boat rental, Lilli whipped out her camera. She snapped pictures of tourists climbing over one another, trying to steady their tipsy rowboats. A middle-aged couple rammed their boat into another, like kids in bumpercars at a carnival. Snap!

Lilli turned when she heard Zack's voice. "Thanks," he said. "If they come back, call Gram Jenkins at Baywatch Inn."

"Did you find out something?" Lilli asked.

"Joe here saw them talking to a man last night around closing time, about eight o'clock."

"Did you know the man?" Lilli asked Joe.

"No. He was a tourist, not a local."

"What makes you say that?"

"Everybody in this town knows everybody else." He turned back to work and Lilli and Zack moved on.

Lilli asked, "Did Joe give you a description?"

"Yeah," Zack said. "But it's not much to work with. Average height, average weight, dark hair. Tan face and arms."

"Maybe somebody else will fill in the details," Lilli said. "Keep trying. I'm starting to get a funny feeling in the pit of my stomach."

"It must be hunger pains." Zack patted his stomach.

"Me too. This sea air sure works up an appetite. How about some lunch?"

"Sure. I read in the Baywatch brochure that the Corner Cafe serves great chowder."

"What are we waiting for?"

It was one-thirty and the Corner Cafe was emptying out. "Sit at a clean table," the waitress called out as she carted away a tray of dirty dishes.

"Thanks, Sally," Zack shot back.

Lilli's eyebrows rose. "How did you—?"

"Her nametag," Zack said. "You don't have to be a detective to notice that."

Lilli felt foolish.

While Zack scanned the menu posted on a chalkboard, Lilli studied his profile. A small scar traveled below the jaw line. Didn't Harrison Ford have a scar, too? Gram's Harrison Ford mania had definitely gotten to her.

Sally sauntered over to their table. "What'll it be?" she asked.

"The special," Zack said. "A cup of clam chowder and a catch-of-the-day sandwich."

"Same for me," Lilli said. "And some crackers, please."

"They come with the chowder," Sally snapped and turned on her heel.

"Hometown syndrome," Zack said. "Locals don't like an outsider telling them how to do their job."

"You sound like an expert."

"I'm from a small town in upstate New York."

"I didn't mean to be rude," Lilli said. "I want the locals on my side. I'll be 'borrowing' their town for the next few days."

"How long are you staying?"

"Until Wednesday."

"Good," Zack said. "I was hoping to see you again, if that's okay."

"Sure," Lilli nodded, trying hard to appear nonchalant. The man–woman thing was one big game and she knew the ground rules. Enthusiasm and eagerness scared off men.

Zack's gaze held hers. "I'm busy tonight with the rehearsal dinner. And tomorrow's the wedding. Maybe we could get together on Monday? There's all kinds of holiday things going on on Monday."

"Great! I'd like that, if you don't mind my snapping photos everywhere we go."

"Do you always put business before pleasure?"

Before Lilli could answer, Sally arrived with their steaming cups of chowder. She dropped a half-dozen packets of oyster crackers in front of Lilli. "That should keep you busy," she said frostily and turned away.

"Ouch!" Lilli said. "She cuts deep."

As they waited for their chowder to cool, their conversation returned to the missing Morgan women and the Baywatch Inn.

"Excuse me," said a pretty dark-haired woman, stepping out of the booth behind them. "I don't mean to eavesdrop, but is there some kind of trouble? My grandmother runs Baywatch Inn and—"

"You must be Annie," Lilli said and introduced herself and Zack.

"Please, come join us," Zack invited.

"Thanks," Annie said. Balancing her iced tea in one hand, and her purse in the other, she slid in next to Zack.

"I saw your paintings," Lilli said. "They're great."

"Thanks. They're from my Montauk collection. The Montauk Indians used to live around here."

"Gram told me," Lilli said.

Annie added, "My husband, Matt, is of Montauk heritage."

"That's what Gram said."

"Gram, the family press agent," Annie said.

"Are you still painting?" Lilli asked as she tasted the chowder.

"Not as much as I'd like to. I'm busy illustrating children's books, and there's always a deadline hanging over my head."

Zack pulled out the picture of Clarissa and Betty Morgan. "Let me fill you in on our mystery," he said. "The Morgans took a room at Gram's and never returned. Gram's letting Lilli stay in your room until she knows if they plan on checking out. The husband is on his way and he doesn't want the police involved, so Gram is abiding by his wishes—at least for now."

"Do you suspect foul play?" Annie asked.

"It may be nothing," Zack said, "or it could be something. A person isn't officially missing until twenty-four hours have elapsed."

"Zack's a detective," Lilli interjected.

"Gram has me under her spell," Zack said. "I'll check back with her later and make sure she's comfortable with what's happening."

"Thanks, I'll drop by and see her too." Annie turned toward Zack. "My husband, Matt, is just like you, very protective of Gram." She shrugged. "What is Gram's secret? She wins over every man who sets foot in the Inn."

"If you find the answer to that question, call me," Lilli said. "I'd like to know and so would my friends."

Annie looked at her watch. "I'd better run. After stopping at Gram's, I'm going to East Bay to visit Matt's Aunt Arabelle. We sketch together or take photographs, just like she and my mother used to do."

Zack said, "I wish I had your talent. I'd like to put on paper the man Joe saw with the Morgan women. It might put Gram's mind at ease."

Determination sparkled in Annie's blue eyes. "I'll give it my best shot, if you'd like. My sketch pad's in my car."

"That would be great," Zack said.

"You two finish your lunch," Annie said. "I'll call Arabelle and tell her I'm running late. I'll get my sketch pad and be back in a flash," she said and hurried out the door.

Twenty minutes later, Lilli and Zack watched as Annie sketched the man Joe described. Joe peered closely at the face emerging in Annie's quick strokes of charcoal. "Good, good," he said encouragingly. "Cheeks a bit more sunken, Annie. Add a few worry lines across his forehead. He's probably thirty to thirty-five."

Joe stepped back and studied the sketch. "You've got it all, Annie girl, except the eyes. The guy had these weird eyes. Wild, like a trapped animal. Those eyes could peel paint off a boat at thirty yards."

Lilli said, "Do you remember anything else? Was the man wearing any jewelry? A wedding ring maybe?"

Joe stroked his chin several times. "No jewelry," he said.

Zack commented, "Lilli has a great eye for detail. Right down to whether a man is married or single."

Lilli ignored the pointed comment. "Joe, you said he was tanned. Anything—"

"These tourists here are putting words in my mouth," Joe muttered to Annie. "I said the man's face and arms were tanned, but his legs were as white as milk. And scrawny as toothpicks."

Annie smiled at Joe. "Lilli and Zack aren't your typical tourists, are they? They've only been in Grayrocks one day and already they're involved in Gram's puzzle. She's really taken them under her wing."

"Well, if Gram gives them her stamp of approval, they've got mine too." He reached out with his huge paw-like hands and pulled Zack and Lilli closer. "Here's the scoop. The man in the sketch has what we call a farmer's tan."

Lilli said, "I'm sorry. I don't get the significance."

Joe sighed. "The guy wears long pants at work. And he works outdoors. That might give you something to go on."

"Thanks. You've been a big help," Zack said. He took the drawing that Annie tore from her sketch pad.

The sketch fluttered in Zack's hands. Dark clouds were gathering and the wind was picking up. People on the beach gathered up their blankets and beach chairs. "Just a few showers blowing in," Joe said, squinting and scanning the waves. "The tourists run at the first drop. They come here to get wet, but they're real particular when it strikes. They only want salt water."

Lilli followed Joe's gaze. Beyond the fishing pier and the swimmers leaving the beach, beyond the jetty, she saw a deserted area about half the size of a football field. "How come no one swims over there at that beach?" she asked.

"That's not a swimming beach," Joe said. "That's Clam Hollow. It's no better than a big hole in the ground. But the Montauk Indians used to go clamming there, and it's kind of sacred to many folks. See that line of gray rocks jutting out into the bay?" Joe pointed into the distance. "That's the jetty. No one swims beyond the jetty because of rip tides."

Annie chuckled. "And plenty of broken shells ready to

attack tender feet. Tourists rarely go there. And locals, never."

Lilli shaded her eyes. "Oh yes. Now I see the NO TRESPASSING sign. Oh, and there's another. And another. Why, they're all over the place." Lilli reached for her field glasses. "There's a red brick building over there in Clam Hollow. It looks like a small garage."

"It was a storage unit for the power company from when they did some work out there," Annie said. "It's been abandoned for at least a year. Talk to Gram about it and watch the feathers fly. It's tops on her list of projects in her 'Beautify Grayrocks' plan. She wants it spruced up or removed."

Lilli studied the building for a few seconds and then snapped her zoom lens onto her camera. "I'll take a few shots, just for the heck of it. It's so alien and nontouristy."

A few raindrops landed on Lilli's face. She took her shots and quickly covered her camera against the rain. "That finishes this roll," she said. "I'm going to take it and some others to be developed. I saw a place near the Corner Cafe."

"I'd recommend Conklin's Photography Shoppe," Annie said. "Mr. Conklin is the friendly type. If the rain keeps up, he'll let you hang out inside. I should warn you, he loves to talk."

"Not too much, I hope. I'm in a rush to see if I need to repeat any shots." She looked one last time at the abandoned brick building. Suddenly, she felt cold, and for reasons she couldn't explain, apprehensive. "I wonder if Mr. Morgan has arrived yet," she said.

"I'm going to Baywatch to find out," Zack said. "Curiosity is getting the better of me."

"Me too," Lilli said and shook off the chill that was

creeping up her spine. "Maybe I'll see you there after I finish at the photo center."

"I'll count on it," Zack said.

He seemed eager to see her again. The feeling was mutual, but she knew better than to wear her heart on her sleeve. Actually, most of her Grayrocks wardrobe consisted of sleeveless tee shirts, so that wasn't a problem.

Chapter Three

Men in Pants

Lilli walked away from the beach, her mind in a jumble about Zack. He was handsome, intelligent, good-natured, and single. She couldn't stop thinking about him. Her mother would be pleased. She could hear Mom's mantra: When are you going to meet a nice man and settle down?

But Mom came from another generation, worlds away. The men Mom remembered were always in hot pursuit. A few dates, and he gave his sweetheart his class ring. Soon after, they got engaged. They married and settled down to a life of, well, that depended on Mom's mood, which often reflected Dad's willingness to pick up his wet towel from the bathroom floor. Mom didn't have a clue about today's men. She couldn't fathom that the mere mention of the word *commitment* sent a man running like an Olympic finalist.

Before she knew it, Lilli was in the center of town. Joe at the bait shops was right about the weather. The rain had already turned to drizzle and the sun was peeking through the clouds. Just ahead on a low-slung green awning, she saw the gold lettering of Conklin's Photography Shoppe.

Music blared when she opened the door and stepped inside. A high soprano voice warbled, "Picture me upon your knee, with tea for two and two for tea." Above the doorframe, Lilli saw a lever that set off the musical interlude.

"Hello," the clerk called out. His nametag read Bud Conklin, identifying him as the owner. Tall, trim, and in his mid-fifties, he wore a baseball cap with the peak turned backward. "Call out if you need my help." Laugh lines creased his angular face.

"Thanks." Lilli picked up a shopping basket, loaded it with several dozen rolls of film, and carried her purchases to the counter. "You keep a well-stocked establishment, Mr. Conklin. I've found everything I need." She set the film down and pulled out the cylinders containing the film she had shot. "I'd like these developed. If it's not too much trouble, could they be ready in an hour?"

Mr. Conklin's eyes grew big. "Woooo-eeeee! I've never had so many rolls of film from one customer at one time. You're not Grayrocks's typical tourist. Are you somebody I should recognize?"

Lilli laughed. "I'm Lilli Masters," she said and plucked her business card from her wallet.

Mr. Conklin studied the pale green card with the chain of white lilies along the border. "A logo that takes advantage of your name. Good eye appeal, too. You'll be easy to remember," he said and rang up her sales.

"I hope so," Lilli said and explained what she was doing in Grayrocks.

"I'm honored that a real professional is using my shop."

He bagged her purchases and dropped in the receipt. "Where are you staying?"

"Baywatch Inn."

He jotted it down on the card she'd given him and taped it to the side of the cash register. "Please give Margaret, uh, I mean Gram, my best."

"She must be a friend of yours," Lilli said. She remembered Annie's comment that Mr. Conklin liked to talk. She would work up to asking him if he had seen a customer with strange, piercing eyes and startled expression.

"Gram's my bridge partner. We have a Monday night game during the low season. That's when we finally have time to think. And Sundays we hit the trails with our cycling club, steering clear of tourists. We take turns picnicking in East Bay, Grayrocks, and Oysterville. East Bay's my favorite. It's an obstacle course of inlets, coves, and one-lane bridges. Very challenging."

Mr. Conklin turned the peak of his baseball cap forward and pointed to the embroidered words *Cycling Nut.* They were surrounded by clusters of real almonds and cashews glued onto the fabric. "Gram made this for me." Lilli imagined Gram surprising him with it during a bike ride. Gram had quite a romantic streak.

Lilli could see the attraction between Gram and Mr. Conklin. Gram ran around Baywatch Inn like a teenager, and Mr. Conklin seemed boyish enough to keep up with her. Apparently, Gram liked younger men. Lilli figured Gram must be about 65, a good ten years older than Mr. Conklin.

"Gram and I've been friends for years," Mr. Conklin said. "Lately, I've stopped calling her Gram and switched to Margaret. You get my drift, don't you?" He winked and set aside Lilli's canisters of film. "Her daughter and son-in-law used to own this shop. They died in a terrible accident, a real tragedy."

"Gram mentioned it to me. I felt so sorry for her, losing both at the same time."

"I didn't think she'd get over it. Thank God she had her granddaughter, Annie. They're quite a team." He cleared his throat. "Anyway, I bought the building, the shop and the upstairs apartment. Gram was real particular about who took over, sentimental reasons and all. She hated to sell, but she couldn't handle Baywatch and the shop. She wanted to spend as much time as possible with Annie."

"I met Annie today," Lilli said. "She's the one who recommended you."

"Annie sends a lot of business my way. Between you and me, I think she likes to keep me busy so I'll stay out of Gram's way. Gram is a woman who likes her space, if you know what I mean. She gets downright ornery if you try and fence her in." He smiled. "It's that old bug-a-boo commitment rearing its ugly head."

Lilli said, "It's refreshing to hear a man say 'commitment' and not leap over the counter and run for the hills."

Mr. Conklin arched forward and massaged his lower back with his knuckles. "No more rain today," he said, changing the subject, as if he realized he was treading in perilous waters.

Lilli ducked to look beneath the outside awning and check out the accuracy of Mr. Conklin's forecast.

"I never doubt what my back tells me," he said rocking back on his heels. "You mark my words, plenty of rain is coming in tomorrow."

Lilli wanted to speed things along. Bubbling in her brain were the words, *Cut the chit-chat and get to the developing*, but she kept silent. Patience was the key. She was getting the knack of communicating around here. Don't tell the locals how to conduct their business. Mention you know someone in town, then stand back. Let them do their job in their own style and time frame.

Lilli killed time by browsing through the selection of photo albums. When she looked up, Mr. Conklin was returning from a back room, separated from the counter area by a curtain. The sounds of running water and humming came through the curtain. "My daughter, Mary Lou, is developing your film," he explained. "I told her it was a rush job." He smiled. "There will be a ten-percent discount. Professional courtesy."

"That's not necessary, but thank you very much. I'll probably have more film to be developed tomorrow."

"We're closed tomorrow," he said. "Monday too, because of the Labor Day holiday. I hate to turn my back on customers, but I promised my daughter we'd go fishing."

"Speaking of customers, did a man come in here yesterday or today, a man with unusual eyes?"

"Unusual, in what way?"

"Kind of weird. Wide-open, startled-looking. Like an animal trapped in headlights."

Mr. Conklin chuckled. "That description fits most of the young bucks around these parts who've been on a late-night toot."

Lilli figured the man that Joe saw talking to Betty and Clarissa Morgan was slightly older than a young buck. "I think I'll wait outside," she said. "I'd like to take more pictures."

"No problem," he said, lifting up a stool. He carried it out the front door and set it by the window. "You're a good advertisement for my shop. Just sit here, focus, and shoot away!" He stood in the doorway for a moment, admiring the camera she selected from the collection in her tote bag. "I'll let you know when your pictures are done," he said and retreated into his shop. The muffled strains of "You ought to be in pictures" wafted through the closing door.

Perched a few feet from the four corners where Main crossed Front Street, Lilli could see the town center. She studied the men who passed by, watching for one in his mid-thirties, wearing shorts, with dark hair and, uh, what did Joe call it? Hmmmm . . . a farmer's tan. Pale legs and tanned arms would give the guy away.

Twenty minutes later when she was about to give up, two perfect candidates came out of Vickory's Hardware Shoppe. Eureka! She grabbed her tote bag, hopped off the stool, and hurried toward them.

Lilli wanted to yank off their sunglasses, but thought she'd try something a bit more subtle. "Excuse me, gentlemen," she said. "I'm conducting a survey for *Viewpoint* magazine. Would you mind showing me the brand name on your sunglasses?"

"Why I'd be honored, ma'am," the taller man said. "My name's Ed. E-D. This here's Sam, S-A-M. Make sure you spell our names right if you quote us." He guffawed and pulled off his glasses.

Without even glancing at Ed's eyes, Lilli knew he wasn't the man she was looking for. Neither was Sam. In her eagerness, she had ignored the obvious. Ed was too tall and Sam too heavy. Just to make sure, Lilli checked out their eyes. Nothing unusual there.

She decided to make the best use of her time. "Do you have time for a few questions?" she asked.

"Yes, ma'am," Ed said. "All we got waiting for us is our wives with their honeydew lists. Honey do this.

Honey do that. They spend all week planning projects for us."

Sam rapped his knuckles against the windowsill. "Thank God for the hardware store. It's our port in the storm."

Ed said, "Some Saturdays we buy wrenches and paint brushes we don't even need, just to get away."

Lilli recognized the grumbling of happily married men. "I'll bet you wear sunglasses because you work outside. Am I right?"

"Yes, ma'am," Ed said. "I work my butt off killing them creepy critters that annoy the folks in Grayrocks."

"Do you mean tourists?" Lilli joked.

"If it was legal, I would. No, ma'am. I'm an exterminator. Termites, not tourists, are my victims."

Lilli turned her tape recorder toward Sam. "And what do you do for a living?"

Sam tucked his thumbs in his belt loops, rocked back on his heels, and said, "I'm with the Public Works department."

"In other words," Ed teased, "he tars roads."

Lilli made a big show of looking at their legs. "I can tell by your pale legs you wear long pants at work."

Ed said, "Would you want them critters creeping up your legs?"

Lilli shook her head vigorously.

Sam chimed in, "Would you want to be hit with flying tar and gravel?"

"I see what you mean. Well, thanks for your help," Lilli said. She was about to leave, when something occurred to her. "I have another article in mind," she fibbed. "It's on men's fashions. Can you think of other professions where men work outdoors in long pants in the summer?"

Sam jerked his thumb toward the door. "Most of the customers in there are wearing long pants."

Lilli gnawed her lip. She had been so foolish, concentrating on men in shorts. The man she was looking for could be wearing long pants. He could have walked right past her.

"Thanks again," Lilli said. She pulled open the door to Vickory's Hardware and stepped inside. It took her a few seconds to adjust to the light. The buzz of conversations stopped mid-sentence. All eyes turned toward her. None of them were deer-trapped-in-headlights eyes. She took a few steps toward the display of stepladders. The men's stone-faced stares told her she had invaded an all-male enclave.

"Excuse me," Lilli said and laughed nervously as she sifted a handful of nails through her fingers. "I made a wrong turn. I was looking for the perfume store." She took a few steps and reached for the doorknob. The clerk at the register snickered. "Sorry, ma'am. We carry toilet water, but not perfume. The Alcove Department Store is your best bet."

"Thank you," Lilli said and hurried out to the sidewalk, with the sounds of laughter ringing in her ears. She returned to her perch in front of Mr. Conklin's shop, determined this time to include shots of men in long pants. The more she watched, the more amazed she became. Grayrocks consisted of parallel universes. Tourists in brand-new shorts—locals in faded shorts or long pants, spattered with paint, stained with grease, grass, or who knows what.

Lilli was busily snapping photos and paid no attention when a man came up behind her, until he grabbed her camera and took off running down the street.

Too surprised to scream, Lilli watched him yank open

her camera, rip out the film, and toss the camera and film into the potted plants clustered outside a shop. That shocked her to her senses. "Stop! Thief!" she called and started running. Elbows pumping, tote bag slapping against her side, she chased after him.

People turned to watch the commotion. One man tried to block the thief's path. Another grabbed hold of his shirt, but the thief knocked him aside and sprinted on across the street, darting through the slow-moving traffic. Horns honked. An irate driver shouted, "Hey, buddy, you wanna get yourself killed?" But the thief was already sprinting around the corner.

Lilli dashed across the street, too, dodging cars and bicycles and mumbling "I'm sorry . . . I'm sorry" to the drivers. When she turned the corner, the thief was no-where in sight. Only then did she realize he was the man Joe had described, the man Annie had sketched. He was average height and weight, dark hair, pale scrawny legs. He was the man she was looking for! What had she done to him that he would want to destroy her photos?

Frustrated and angry, Lilli retraced her steps to the pot-ted plants lined up beneath the hand-painted sign on the window of Flora's Florist Shoppe. A large woman wear-ing a floral-print smock, matching visor, and threadbare pink sneakers, stood in front of the plants. She held a pink watering can in one hand and a roll of film, dangling like an overworked yo-yo in the other.

"I'm Flora," she said. "I saw him. He was spittin' mad and he ruined your film on purpose. What did you do, take a picture of him with somebody's wife?"

Lilli shook her head. "I don't think I took any pictures of him." It suddenly dawned on her. He wanted to destroy something on that film. "Must be the heat," she said and forced herself to laugh.

"Must be," Flora said.

"By any chance did you find my camera?" Lilli asked.

"No. But it's here somewhere. We'll find it."

"Could I trouble you for a plastic bag?" Lilli asked.

"Sure. Be right back."

Lilli poked through the pots, carefully moving dahlia leaves and blossoms aside. She found the camera in the fourth pot.

"Here you go," Flora said, huffing up.

"Thanks." Lilli plunged her hand into the plastic bag and gingerly picked up the camera. She tied the bag shut and dropped it into her tote bag. She saw Flora's quizzical look. "I'm making sure I don't lose any of the parts," Lilli fibbed. She hoped the man had left a good set of fingerprints on the camera.

"Stealing your camera. Ruining your film. In broad daylight, no less. What is this town coming to?" Flora remarked.

Lilli pressed her business card into Flora's hand. "If you see that man again, please call me. I'm staying with Gram Jenkins at Baywatch Inn."

"You're in good hands," Flora said. "Oops! There goes my telephone." She hurried into her shop.

A panicky feeling overwhelmed Lilli. She took a few deep gulps of fresh air to clear her head. Could that man have gone into Conklin's Photography Shoppe and somehow gotten his hands on her photos? She started to run. The words "No. Please no," stuck in her throat.

Mr. Conklin opened the door before her hand reached the knob. "Where have you been?" he asked to the accompanying strains of music. "Your photos have been ready for a long time."

"They're still here?" Lilli tried to catch her breath.

"Of course. We don't send out our work. It's all done

on the premises. By the way, my daughter has something to tell you. She's been waiting for you."

"Sorry I held things up," Lilli said, looking at her watch. "I appreciate the rushing you and your daughter did to get my photos developed." She hadn't realized how much time had flown by. She wanted to return to Baywatch Inn, to think things through. Should she take the camera to the police? Should she ask Gram's advice? Yes, that was better. She'd discuss things with Gram. She'd ask Zack's opinion too, meet Mr. Morgan, and figure out what the heck was going on.

"This is my daughter, Mary Lou," Mr. Conklin said, ushering Lilli inside. "She's home for the long weekend from Andrews University. She likes to help out in the shop when she can."

"Yeah, right." Mary Lou pouted. "Dad and I are supposed to be fishing. He promised to close up early, but he always puts his customers first." She looked very much like her father. The same big-boned physique, high cheekbones, and rosy complexion.

"I'm sorry I ruined your plans," Lilli said. "I'll take my photos and be on my way."

Mary Lou huffed, "Now that you're here, what's another couple of minutes. Dad said you were asking about a man with strange eyes. I've seen him. He had creepy eyes that bore a hole right through you. He came in here yesterday while Dad was busy on the phone."

"Gram called," Mr. Conklin said. "So I stopped everything, and . . . Sorry, go on."

"Did he buy anything?" Lilli asked.

"A Polaroid camera."

"Did he pay by credit card?"

"No, cash."

"Polaroid—" Lilli thought out loud. "Good if you want instant results."

"Yeah," Mary Lou replied. "And total control. There's no developer involved. No one but you sees them, unless you say so."

For the second time that day, a cold chill ran up Lilli's spine. "Did you notice anything else unusual about the man?"

Mary Lou nodded. "The first joint of his index finger on his left hand is missing."

"I wonder how that happened," Lilli murmured.

"An accident maybe. Or a knife fight."

Chapter Four

Mr. Morgan

Lilli hurried toward Baywatch Inn. She knew the strap of her tote bag traversing her chest made her look like a crossing guard at a schoolyard, but there was no time to be worried about fashion. She was playing it safe. No sneak was going to run off with her photos. She had learned the hard way. Just to be safe, she looked over her shoulder every few steps, half-expecting the dark-haired man to be barreling down the street and gaining on her.

Looking again, she noticed a dark green Miata convertible at the stop sign. She did a double take. It was Zack driving. Next to him, practically in his lap, sat a pretty young woman, tilting back her head, smiling at him. No, not smiling. Grinning from ear to ear and probably laughing at every amusing word Zack uttered. She could package that syrupy sweetness and give Nutri-Sweet a run for its money!

Lilli kept her eyes fixed on the woman, hoping Zack

wouldn't turn his head and notice her. Her pale blond hair glinted in the late afternoon sunshine, set off by her navy-blue dress with spaghetti straps. Perky, that was how Lilli would describe her. Well-groomed, too. Her straight hair cascaded from the chiseled side part and was anchored neatly behind her ears. She could be arrested for impersonating one of the blond TV newscasters.

At this point, Lilli had already made two decisions. She would look through all the photos to see if there was anything, anything at all, that the man might have wanted and she would store the negatives in a safe place. As she turned the final corner, she made another decision. She would find out who that blond bombshell was and what she was doing with Zack Faraday. Jealousy had struck with the ferocity of a high-school crush. Yet what right did she have to be jealous? She had only known Zack for a few hours. Apparently the blond in the Miata had known him much, much longer. Blonds! They—

"Helllloooooo!" Gram greeted Lilli with a wave of her hammer. She was on her knees on the front porch, nailing down some loose boards. Pushing herself up, she said, "Lilli girl, you look a bit under the weather. A nice hot shower and you'll be good as new. I know the locals can be rough on tourists, but you look like you've been pulled through a knot-hole."

"It's a long story."

"That's my favorite kind," Gram said, steering Lilli to one of the rocking chairs by the railing. Lilli dropped onto the plump yellow cushion, stretched out her long slender legs, and sighed with relief.

Gram plunked down in the rocking chair next to Lilli's. She rocked back and forth several times, then hugged her knees to her chin. "You have to understand, Lilli, the tourists are our entertainment. Summer TV is nothing but re-runs, so we invent our own shows. 'Get The Tourists' is our best one. By the second day, we ease up. Sometimes we forget ourselves and turn downright friendly. But don't let on to anybody I told you so. Why, before you could say 'fried flounder' I'd be on the outs with everybody."

"Not with Bud Conklin."

Gram's work boots struck the floor with a vengeance. The rocking chair almost flipped. "What's he been telling you?"

"Not much. I'm good at reading between the lines."

"Well, here's the bottom line. His daughter, Mary Lou, and my granddaughter, Annie, are only a few years apart. Mary Lou is very possessive and can't stand the thought of anyone replacing her mother, so she's been spreading stories about me. I've had my flirty moments, I don't deny that. But now, according to the scuttlebutt Mary Lou's been circulating, I'm robbing the cradle."

Gram resumed rocking as if it were a competitive sport. Then she slowed down and smiled. "I'm good at reading between the lines, too. Zack didn't say so, but I know he's falling for you."

"Open your eyes, Gram. He's fallen for someone else. I saw Zack and a drop-dead gorgeous blond with a perky smile straight out of a toothpaste ad. They were a few blocks from here in a convertible. They didn't even notice me, that's how busy they were gazing into each other's eyes."

"I'll bet she's a bridesmaid. He's probably accompanying her to the rehearsal dinner. Mark my words, Zack is sweet on you."

"So you're calling him Zack, not Harrison."

"I'm going along with what he thinks is best. He's checking out Grayrocks for his next location." She chuckled and gave Lilli a knowing look. "He's a major star, you know, gets his say in all aspects of a film. I read that in a magazine in Pick 'n' Pay while waiting in line to buy peaches. Forget that. Zack left a note for you. He said it was important, so we'd better see what he has to say." She rocked forward and, in one fluid movement, landed by the screen door.

"I need a favor," Lilli stammered, following Gram into the lobby. "Is there a police officer you could recommend? I might want to talk to someone official."

Gram said, "Give me the names of the locals you've encountered. I'll have a word with them. They've been playing hard and fast with you. They did the same to Annie's husband, Matt, but their guff made him stronger. You look like you're ready to crumble."

"It's not the locals," Lilli explained. "Did Zack and Annie tell you about the man that was seen talking to Betty and Clarissa Morgan?"

"Yeah, they showed me the sketch."

"That man is trouble. I'm not sure exactly what he's up to, but—"

"Zack and Annie don't seem to think there's anything to be concerned about, and I agree. Ralph Morgan arrived and explained a few things. I'll fill you in, but first, what makes you think this man is trouble?"

"He ran off with one of my cameras and exposed a roll of film. For whatever reason, he didn't want me to see the photos. But he might not know that I shot dozens of rolls of film. It's possible the picture he wanted to destroy is right here in my tote bag."

Gram frowned. "Any clue as to who he is?"

"No, but Mary Lou Conklin remembers him coming in to her shop. Flora saw him too. I saved the camera, hoping the police can find a good set of fingerprints."

"We'll call my friend Hank, the Chief of Police. You report the theft and he'll see about those prints. He'll take statements from Flora and Mary Lou too. Hank's real good at interviewing witnesses. He learns his techniques from 'Law and Order.' He never misses an episode. He'll treat a hit-and-run in Grayrocks the same way those New York detectives handle murders and muggings. Well, enough about Hank. Let me look at you. You look all trembly. Did that man hurt you? Did he threaten you?"

"No," Lilli said, "and I feel much better already, just from talking to you. But to be on the safe side, I'd like to store the negatives in your safe."

"No problem," Gram said. "Just follow me."

Before they could get away, the screen door slammed shut. A short heavy-set man in brown shorts and tan shirt, soaked with perspiration, lumbered into the lobby. He swiped at his brow with his handkerchief.

"Why, hello, Mr. Morgan," Gram said. "Everything okay?"

"Why wouldn't it be?" he muttered and headed toward the stairs. "I came back for my hat. With all these questions from everybody, I forgot my hat. The sun's burning a hole in my head."

"Have a nice day, Mr. Morgan," Gram said. She blinked her eyes at Lilli in an exaggerated way, signaling, Lilli surmised, that she was being sarcastic.

Mr. Morgan reached for the banister and rested his full weight against it. "The elevator's too hot and crowded," he muttered and started up the stairs.

Gram confided to Lilli. "Zack figures this disappearing act by Mrs. Morgan has happened before. He's guessing it's a cat and mouse game they play."

"And Zack is an expert in husband and wife games?"

Gram waved away Lilli's question with the back of her

hand. "Mr. Morgan admitted that his wife gets these moods, 'bad spells' he called them, and she runs off, claiming she needs a breath of fresh air. These spells started shortly after her older daughter died, and apparently they've gotten worse. If you've ever suffered the overwhelming grief of losing a child, you'd understand the strange behavior that can overtake you."

Lilli nodded. "Zack may have a point."

Gram cleared her throat. "Zack figures Mrs. Morgan sets up her husband to make him jealous. She's probably sitting in some comfortable inn waiting for him to find her. No doubt she knows, from previous experience, that she won't be reported missing until twenty-four hours have passed. That gives her until about eight o'clock tonight. So she has a few hours to make her husband squirm. Even if this has nothing to do with grief, you have to admit people are strange critters. You work with the public, too, so you know that as well as I do."

"But what about the daughter?" Lilli asked. "Why would she go along with this jealousy routine?"

"I don't know," Gram said. "We didn't get around to that. Besides, you can only poke so far into someone's life. Then you have to back off."

Lilli frowned. "Something's not right about all this. Do the police know the women might be missing?"

"No," Gram said. "Mr. Morgan insisted he could handle this. For now, I'm going along with his decision— and I know what you're thinking. But it's got nothing to do with bad publicity for Baywatch Inn. It's the first rule of good business: the customer is always right. Being a naturally curious person, I'm keeping my eye on the situation and if anything suspicious happens—"

"Like a large trunk being carried to his car—"

"Yes, something like that. Then I'll step in." She laughed. "You've got a vivid imagination."

"It comes from watching so many movies," Lilli said.

"Smart aleck," Gram teased. She walked behind the counter and into her office. "You probably think there's a safe behind one of Annie's paintings." She swept her arms in a full circle, taking in all four walls, all covered with Annie's Montauk scenes. "That's how they do it in the movies. But not me. Everybody's wise to that old trick."

Gram closed the door behind her and locked it. She walked over to her desk, pushed aside the chair on wheels that rolled from her computer to her filing cabinets. "Wait until you see this," she said. She knelt amid the pale-blue sailboats bobbing in a navy-blue sea that patterned the carpet.

Gram chuckled. "The look on someone's face when they see where my safe is hidden is precious. Of course, only Annie, Matt, Bud Conklin, and a few other dear and trusted friends know about it."

"Gram, you hardly know me. Are you sure you should be doing this?"

"Women's intuition," Gram said. "I know in my heart you can be trusted." She peered over her glasses at Lilli. "Prove me wrong and I'll chase you to hell and back."

Gram grabbed two corners of the plastic runner and began rolling it up. Midway, she slowed and exclaimed, "Thar she blows!" A rectangle of carpeting the size of a medicine cabinet lifted. It was attached to the plastic runner. "Nobody's going to find your negatives here," Gram said beaming with pride. She reached up, took the key from her desk drawer, poked it into the keyhole, and gave it one quick turn. The door to the safe sprung open.

"Ingenious," Lilli said.

"It's one of Bud Conklin's inventions," Gram explained. "Since his Muriel died, he's kept himself busy."

Lilli passed Gram the envelopes filled with negatives. "Thanks. This is a load off my mind." She massaged her neck, working out the kinks. "I think I'll take that hot shower you mentioned."

"You'll be staying on in Annie's room," Gram said. "Mr. Morgan requested his wife's room and I couldn't say no. I hope you don't mind. Enjoy your shower and then have supper with me."

"I can't impose any further."

"Nonsense. I have enough scallops to sink a ship. And some left-over Waldorf salad from the lunch crowd. Did I mention my blueberry pie, topped with vanilla ice cream?"

Lilli held up her hand. "Stop! You win."

Gram checked her watch. "Give me two hours to settle down the dinner crowd and then we'll rip into those scallops."

"Great," Lilli said. "That will give me time to check through my photos."

Gram slapped her thigh. "Aren't we forgetting something? Come on, Zack's letter is waiting. He wrote it on my Baywatch stationery. What a catch!"

"You mean Zack?"

"No, his signature. Harrison Ford's signature!"

Leaning against the reception counter, Lilli carefully opened the envelope and passed it to Gram. Zack's handwriting was bold, sloping across the page, with the dots from the i's and the crosses from the t's missing their mark. Lilli figured he must have been in a big hurry to meet his charming blond.

"Well?" Gram asked. "What's cooking?"

"He wants me to meet him after the rehearsal dinner for a drink. Ten o'clock at the Soundshore Lodge."

"Whooah, girl! He has romance on his mind." Gram's eyes sparkled. "Bud Conklin and I had our first official date there. Mary Lou was at her senior prom. Bud figured she'd never find out. But a missing boutonniere and— Well, that's another story. Anyway, it's a very romantic place. It's at the end of that narrow winding road that hugs the coastline, up High Point Drive."

Gram sighed. "You've seen how calm Grayrocks Bay is. Wait until you see the Long Island Sound at night. There's a deck across the back of the lodge. It's a perfect movie setting with waves crashing against rocks. Zack's probably checking it out for his film. You can lean against the railing and watch the moonlight streak across the water." She toyed with her bangs. "Take my advice, Lilli. Put on a vampy outfit and high heels and show Zack that blonds aren't the only ones who know how to have fun."

"I'll keep it in mind."

Lilli was halfway to her room when she reached into her tote bag, checking for the hundredth time that the photos were still there. Her fingertips grazed a jagged metal edge. The key to the Morgans' room. She had never returned it to Gram.

Lilli took a few more steps, but she couldn't resist. She turned back and went up the main staircase, turned left and stopped outside the Morgans' room. Tiptoeing closer, she pressed her ear to the door.

Strange noises, like whimpers from a wounded animal, came through the door. Then she heard the unmistakable honking sound of someone blowing his nose. Someone was crying. Ralph Morgan? Lumbering steps inside the room came toward the door. She turned and nonchalantly walked down the hallway, willing herself not to run. She heard a door open and looked over her shoulder. Ralph Morgan stepped into the hallway, closed the door, and locked it. He headed toward the stairs and never looked her way.

When the sound of his footsteps receded, Lilli hurried back to his room. She looked both ways to be sure no one was watching as she pushed the key into the lock. The door opened and she slipped inside. She gasped out loud and backed into the door. Photographs. Dozens of photographs. Photographs of Betty Morgan. They lined the bureau, the windowsill, the nightstand, and the headboards of both twin beds. Talk about obsession! A chill ran up Lilli's spine. The room looked just like the shrines you read about that serial killers keep of their victims.

Lilli glanced around. One of the beds was turned down for the night. A black negligee, nipped in at the waist and bowed out at the hips, rested, like a sleeping woman, flowing from below the pillow midway down the bed.

All other traces of Betty and Clarissa Morgan's clothing was gone. Possibly they'd been moved to the dresser drawer, or maybe to the weekender-size suitcase at the foot of the bed.

Lilli heard footsteps in the hallway. She froze. They grew louder, coming closer. She couldn't get caught like this. How could she possibly explain herself? She fled into the bathroom. Please, don't let there be any bodies here, she prayed, shoving aside the shower curtain. She jumped into the bathtub and held her breath. Peeking through the opening between the curtain and the wall, she could see part of the room, including the mirror over the dresser.

The door opened and she heard Mr. Morgan's leather sandals flapping against the hardwood floor. He walked toward the bed with the negligee. In the mirror, she saw him pick up the suitcase. It landed heavily on the bed. He

snapped the hinges open and rummaged through the suitcase. It snapped shut and she heard it plunked down at
the foot of the bed.

Mr. Morgan passed by the doorway, holding a stack of
handkerchiefs. He shoved several in his pockets. So that's
what he had come back for. He had them. He would leave.
She could escape.

Mr. Morgan stopped, sat down on the bed, and blew
his nose. "Please, Betty," he whispered. "Please come
back. I can't take this any more." He whimpered softly.
The depth of his despair brought tears to Lilli's eyes. She
regretted having set foot inside the Morgans' room. She
had invaded their privacy and their grief.

The door slammed shut. Lilli breathed again and vowed
to give up her new career of breaking and entering. She
would never admit to Gram or anyone else her insensitiv-
ity to other people's feelings.

Chapter Five

The Photographs

Still damp from her shower, and still shaking from her experience in Mr. Morgan's room, Lilli wrapped herself in her terry robe. She sat on the bed and opened the stack of envelopes to spread her photos around the comforter. The batch of photos brought back an old familiar fear. A frightening incident had occurred when she was twelve years old, living with her parents and eight-year-old brother, Pete, in Brooklyn.

Her neighbor, Mrs. Lawrence, a professional photographer, had given her a camera for her birthday. For several months, she had taught Lilli about balance, harmony, and arrangement. As a special treat, she occasionally allowed Lilli to use her basement dark room. One Saturday morning, Lilli put on her headset to enjoy her favorite rock music, and set to work developing her negatives.

Forgetting that Lilli was in the house, Mrs. Lawrence locked all the doors and went shopping. As a matter of

habit, she locked the door to the darkroom to protect her
expensive equipment and irreplaceable negatives.

Lilli finished her work and found the door locked. Pan-
icked, she screamed for someone to let her out, but there
was no one to hear. Two hours later, Mrs. Lawrence returned home and found Pete on her front doorstep asking
where his sister was. Pete later recounted that Mrs.
Lawrence shouted, 'Oh, no!' dropped both bags of gro-
ceries, and ran to the dark room, with him at her heels.
They opened the door and found Lilli, slumped in a corner, limp and sobbing, a complete mess. Lilli never again
went into a small confined space that could be locked,
unless she had the key.

Remembering that moment, Lilli touched the Swiss
Army knife that dangled from her tote bag. The all-in-
one tool-kit knife was a high-school graduation gift from
Pete. When she pulled away the tissue, he had shifted
from one foot to the other and said "in case I can't be
there to rescue you from scary places, you'll be able to
rescue yourself."

Turning her attention to the photos, Lilli realized that
Zack reminded her of Pete. They shared a zest for life,
were fun to be with, and could be relied on. At first
glance, the photos looked great. Lilli breathed a sigh of
relief. She counted. None were missing. Many seemed
excellent, exactly what she was looking for. Lilli worked
her way through the batch, setting aside those that were
only adequate. There were no shots of the man who had
run off with her camera.

She came to the pictures of the jetty, Clam Hollow, and
the brick storage building. Her jaw tightened. Some would
have to be re-shot. A small red streak near the building
spoiled all three photos.

She looked more closely. Maybe it was her imagination. The streak was in a slightly different spot in each one, but she had taken them only seconds apart. Could something be wrong with her camera? Lilli reached for her magnifying glass and studied them under the bright light on Annie's desk. She couldn't tell what had caused the streak. Maybe a candy wrapper, a shred of plastic from a child's water wings, something had flown by as she made the shots. Tomorrow morning, she would return to the area, and re-shoot the building with a different camera. On Tuesday, she would ask Mr. Conklin to check out the camera to see if he could determine what caused the red flash.

"Lilli, dinner's ready." Gram's melodic voice traveled down the hallway from the kitchen.

"Coming," Lilli called back. She threw on her jeans and a tee shirt and hurried to Gram's cozy family kitchen. The overhead light, a replica of a ship's steering wheel with a light positioned at each spoke, shone on the honey-brown paneling that covered the walls. A soft golden glow throughout the room lulled Lilli into forgetting about the nerve-jangling experiences of the day.

"Just like old times," Gram greeted Lilli and plunked down two platters, overflowing with fish, string beans, and salad. Lilli took a seat in front of one of the platters and Gram sat across from her in front of the other. "Annie and I used to have supper here every night. We solved the world's problems first and then got down to our own."

Lilli laughed. "Could we skip straight to our own?" She set the three photos in front of Gram and speared a scallop with her fork.

"Try my own special tartar sauce," Gram said, sliding a tiny ceramic pot toward her.

"Mmmmm. Delicious," Lilli said, sampling the sauce. She speared another scallop and dunked it in the sauce as she pointed to the photos. "Any idea what that red streak might be?"

Gram squinted. "Looks like a ribbon. Maybe the tail of a kite? I hope no children were playing out there. It's very dangerous. There have been ten drownings that I can recall in Grayrocks. Eight of them occurred near that jetty. I've told the town council we need a lifeguard stationed there. And that brick building is a real eye sore. I'm working on getting rid of it through the Beautify Grayrocks Committee."

Lilli savored the salad, trying to figure out the distinctive flavor.

"Lime juice, that's my secret ingredient," Gram said, as if reading her mind.

"I'd like the recipe," Lilli said.

"I don't write them down. They're all in my head." She laughed. "Crowding my brain!"

Lilli said, "Maybe we could do a photo shoot about meals at Baywatch Inn. You know, photographs of you and your staff, the food, and your happy guests. I'd like some down-home touches to add to my layout for *Viewpoint* magazine."

"I'm available," Gram said. "Let me know when. I could prepare some of my specialties, like clam fritters and beet salad."

"Let's plan on Tuesday when the crowds have gone. Tomorrow morning, bright and early, I'm going to the jetty to re-shoot."

Gram set down her fork. "Wear old sneakers and work gloves. There's broken shells all over the place and barnacles on the jetty." She sipped her iced tea. "Can I ask a special favor?"

"Anything," Lilli said. "I'm in your debt."

"Take some photos for me. I'll use them for my arguments to beautify Grayrocks." She salted her beans. "I called Hank for you. He's planning on stopping by to see you tomorrow. If you're not here, I'll send him down to the beach. Just watch for his green police cruiser."

"I hope I'm not overreacting," Lilli said.

"Of course not. Set your mind at ease."

Lilli and Gram lingered over dinner, enjoying each other's company. Lilli asked about Grayrocks' history and Gram supplied fact and fancy about the days when pirates, whalers, and bootleggers roamed the waters and the Montauk Indian chief, Wyandanch, conducted ceremonies in Clam Hollow. Finally, Gram pushed away from the table and said, "It's time for dessert." She slid a pie out of the refrigerator and took two dishes from the cabinet.

Lilli cleared away the dinner dishes. "Your granddaughter Annie is great. That was nice of her to sketch the man for us."

Gram topped off the two huge wedges of blueberry pie with orange-sized scoops of vanilla ice cream. "She's the apple of my eye. Or should I say, the blueberry!"

Lilli laughed. "I felt guilty about pulling Annie away from her plans. She said something about visiting her husband's aunt in East Bay."

"Arabelle Revington," Gram said, setting the plates on the table. "Arabelle and my Annie are fast friends. I know this may sound crazy, but at times, I'm just a tad jealous of their relationship." She pulled up her chair in front of the pie. "Then I remind myself that Arabelle and my daughter, Caitlin, that's Annie's mother, had a wonderful friendship that enriched Caitlin's life. For that, I'm thankful."

Gram spooned the melting ice cream into her mouth and savored every drop. "Arabelle and Caitlin enjoyed an hour or so every week with their cameras, shooting out at Arabelle's estate. Photography was Caitlin's profession. For Arabelle, it was a pleasurable pastime. She knew Caitlin wasn't wealthy and couldn't afford to spend time away from her camera shop, so she pretended to be interested in photography and paid Caitlin for lessons. She enjoyed Caitlin's company. I understood that just as I understand the bond between Arabelle and Annie. As they sketch, they share their memories of Annie's mother. I'm not shut out. They tell me, each in their own way, what they talked about. I enjoy the double dose of memories. Photography and sketching are like the sewing circle and quilting bee of bygone days. It's an excuse to be together and talk."

Lilli enjoyed Gram's reminiscences, but she kept checking her watch. She didn't want to be late for her date with Zack. "I'll do the dishes," Lilli said as she finished her last mouthful of pie.

"We'll do them together," Gram said. "It's like I was saying, an excuse to get together and talk."

Side by side at the sink, they washed and dried the dishes and then cleaned up the kitchen.

Lilli hung the dishtowel on the rack and rang out the sponges. "I'd better change into something more respectable."

"Something more sexy, remember," Gram suggested.

"You're bad," Lilli said.

Lilli checked herself in the full-length mirror on the back of Annie's closet door. The white sandals would have to do. She didn't have a vampy outfit with her, but green was her best color. She smoothed her green silky top and adjusted the belt to her white twill pants. The top played up her eyes and the pants fit just right. Not too tight, not too loose. She brushed her cheeks with rouge and spritzed some perfume on her throat. This was a beach town, but she didn't want to appear too casual. She wished she had brought a fancier outfit along. Zack would be coming from a dinner party. He would be well dressed. She realized how much she looked forward to seeing him.

Driving away from town, Lilli turned onto Soundshore Road. Bright lights reflected off her rearview mirror. She squinted and moved her head, trying to avoid the glare. She pressed her foot on the gas pedal and sped down the road. The lights glared in her mirror. She slowed down and signaled for him to pass. He slowed down and stayed behind her. She made out the vehicle. It was a pale gray pickup truck. A man was driving. In the dark, she couldn't make out his features. He bumped into her Bronco. She jerked forward and pulled toward the center of the road. He bumped her again, harder.

Lilli jammed her foot on the accelerator and sped off. Come on, come on, she thought. Where's that turn-off road? She traveled another three miles, her hands gripping the wheel, her breath coming in short spurts. There, she saw the sign, High Point Drive, and the snaky arrow indicating the hair-pin curves. She waited until the last possible moment, and then veered right. Her Bronco bounced and her head nearly hit the roof. She straightened the wheel, bringing the Bronco under control, her eyes glued to the curving road. She blinked away the perspiration dripping into her eyes and breathed a sigh of relief. The truck hadn't followed her. Her imagination was playing tricks.

Suddenly, she heard the sound of gravel crunching. She looked in her rearview mirror. The pickup truck careened onto High Point Drive. Gravel flew. The pickup truck skidded into the ditch.

Lilli jerked to a stop in front of the Soundshore Lodge. She jumped out, ran up the steps, and hurried inside. A quick look at her watch showed ten-twenty. She hoped Zack would arrive soon. What if he didn't show up? She wasn't going out to that parking lot alone.

"Table for one?" the hostess greeted Lilli.

"Two," Lilli said, her voice shaking.

"A quiet booth in the rear?"

"That would be fine," Lilli said and kept her eyes glued to the door.

Lilli sat down. She counted to ten to calm her nerves. She pulled out her compact mirror. Even in the flickering candlelight she could see what a total disaster she was. Her mascara smeared, her lipstick eaten away. She didn't know whether to laugh or cry. Some sexy babe she had turned out to be! The blond in the convertible had nothing to fear from her.

The door swung open and Lilli held her breath. Please let it be Zack, she thought.

Zack sauntered into the lobby and spoke to the hostess. They chatted for a moment and the hostess playfully tapped his shoulder with the menus.

Lilli jumped up from the booth and dashed toward Zack. "I'm so glad to see you," she said. She tugged at his coat sleeve. "Come back here where we can't be seen."

Zack smiled and allowed himself to be led toward the booth. "Is there a jealous husband I should know about?" he asked playfully.

"No," Lilli stammered, sliding onto the bench.

"I see you've been swimming again," he said and she realized her silk shirt was soaked with perspiration.

Chapter Six

Soundshore Lodge

"Someone followed me here." The words caught in Lilli's throat as she fought back tears.

Zack pressed her trembling hands together and held them. "Calm down and tell me what happened," he said. His strong hands were so reassuring. The cold fear of panic churning in Lilli's stomach turned to a warm tingling sensation that swept through her.

The waitress came to the table. "Would you care for something to drink?" she asked. "We have a special red wine, a Merlot, that's been very popular tonight."

Zack said, "Sounds good to me. Lilli?"

She nodded and Zack said, "Two glasses of Merlot, please." As soon as the waitress left, Zack gazed into Lilli's eyes. "Now where were we?"

Lilli told him everything that had happened from the time she left Baywatch Inn until she'd arrived at the

Soundshore Lodge. "It's not my imagination," she said as if she doubted that Zack would believe her.

"You definitely saw a man in a pickup truck," Zack said. "Just as I swung into the parking lot, he was pulling away. He almost crashed into me as he backed out and then shot forward in a hail of gravel. I doubt there's any rubber left on his tires."

"Are you sure he's gone?"

"I'll check the parking lot if it will make you feel better. I'll be right back."

"Be careful," Lilli said. "He's crazy or dangerous or both."

"Don't worry, I run into his type every day at work."

"Right. You're a detective."

"Don't tell Gram. She and I are sharing a great fantasy life. She actually stood on the stairs at Baywatch Inn, struck a sexy pose, and said in a dead-ringer Betty Davis voice, 'Fasten your seatbelt, it's going to be a bumpy ride.' "

Lilli laughed. The tension of the last half-hour flew out the window. While Zack was gone, Lilli checked out the surroundings. There were more people than she had realized, but it was a great place to meet. Everyone snuggled in booths, lost in their private conversations.

Every now and then, the porch door opened and the sound of crashing waves wafted across the room. The couples who wandered in reached up to smooth their wind-blown hair and then resumed holding hands. Lilli breathed deeply and settled back in the booth. As Gram said, this was definitely a place with romance in the air. Lilli would welcome romance into her life. There had been no one special for a long time.

Her heart had been broken two years ago. Dumped, was the word her best friend Sue used when they talked about

Dr. Jeffrey Stone. 'Jeffrey did you a favor,' Sue said. Lilli winced, remembering Jeffrey's harsh words and haughty attitude the night he told her he no longer loved her. He said she embarrassed him by dropping by his office dressed like a truck driver or a punk rocker. He'd make a big show of admiring women in conservative suits and tailored blouses, his idea of professional dress. He didn't want to hear Lilli's explanation, that she dressed the way she did to put her subjects at ease and encourage them to be themselves.

The news had nearly knocked Lilli off her feet. Jeff had dropped her for Tiffany, his new office assistant. Couldn't he have had the decency to fall for an accountant, lawyer, or financial consultant—professional, for gosh sakes. Someone prim and proper in plain pumps to fit his business-like image? Tiffany sat in his swanky suite of offices, amazed that the glitter on her red nail polish didn't budge when she touched a computer key. When Tiffany figured out how to work the electric pencil sharpener, Lilli expected to read about it in the office bulletin.

Betrayed and humiliated, Lilli had shied away from eligible men until now. She definitely felt ready to jump back into the pond and swim to the other side. That was her friend Sue's description of the dating game.

Lilli wondered if Zack was as attracted to her as she was to him. Probably not. This was the real world, not the movies. Nothing that involved emotions ever fell into place so easily or so fast. At least, that had been her experience so far. What fueled the male–female attraction thing anyway? Chemistry—maybe it was as simple as the right combination of estrogen, testosterone, neurotransmitters, whatever. Or could it be astrology? No, that was just hooey. But she was a "moon child" and she usually attracted Taurus and Aries men. She might pull out the oldest line in the world, "What sign are you?"

Lilli sighed contentedly. Geography, that was Sue's theory. Meeting the right man meant being in the right place at the right time. Here he was. Here she was. Two strangers, meeting for the first time in a relaxed resort town at a happy time in their lives. Zack was in Grayrocks to attend his cousin's wedding and she was on a fabulous Labor Day photo assignment. Unfortunately, there was also some crazy nut on the loose.

The waitress set down the drinks. Zack was right behind her. "No truck," he reported, sliding onto the seat. "And nobody hanging around. Let's give him the benefit of the doubt. He's got this thing for pretty redheads. He didn't intend to hurt you. He wanted you to stop so he could meet you." He clinked the rim of his wineglass against hers.

Lilli set down her glass. "I think he was trying to scare me."

"Then he's a fool or a nut-case," Zack said.

"There's something you should know." Lilli told Zack about the camera incident in town and the witnesses who had seen the man. "I'm sure the driver of the pickup truck is the same man who took my camera and the same one who spoke to Betty and Clarissa Morgan before they disappeared. I think he may have hurt them."

"And I think your imagination is working overtime, Lilli. The Morgans will turn up. It's a game of hide and seek. Right now, Mrs. Morgan and her daughter are hiding. Mr. Morgan is seeking. He's done it before, and, from what he confided in me, man to man, he's resigned to doing it again. He says it has to do with his wife's running away from the older daughter's death. She can't accept what happened and this is how she deals with it. He was very convincing. I believe him."

Lilli said, "I can accept that Betty Morgan is playing games with her husband, but I don't think she would drag her daughter into it. And I don't think a teenage girl would go along with it." She sipped her wine. "There's a connection between the man in the truck and the Morgans and me, but I can't figure out exactly what."

She didn't mention her theory that there was a photo or photos in her tote bag back at Baywatch Inn that the man didn't want anyone to see. And she didn't admit that she had searched through them for some kind of condemning evidence and had come up empty-handed. She could see that Zack was impressed by facts, not wild suppositions. "I might have his fingerprints on my camera. Hank, the chief of police, is coming by tomorrow. I'll be curious to see what he can dig up."

"That's a good idea," Zack said. "And, to be on the safe side, follow your instincts about this guy in the truck. Don't go anywhere alone. Stay with crowds, where you can call for help if you need it."

"Then you do think there's danger?"

"Just be cautious is all I'm saying."

She toyed with the stem of her wineglass. "I'm sorry to drag you into all this. You're on vacation. The last thing you need is police work."

"No problem." He reached across the table and entwined her fingers in his. "Well, there is a slight problem. You're impossible to hold hands with. You're shaking. You should slip out of that wet shirt," he said. "Here, take my jacket." He pulled off his jacket and handed it to her.

"Thanks," Lilli said. "Excuse me while I go to the ladies' room."

The hostess caught up to Lilli in the lobby. "I was just

headed for your table, but you've saved me the trip. I have something for you." She held out a pale-blue envelope and winked. "A certain gentleman asked me to give this to you."

Lilli took the envelope and immediately noticed the Baywatch Inn return address. "Thanks," she told the hostess and continued toward the ladies' room. Zack and his notes, Lilli thought. She'd had two or three serious relationships and a few not so serious. Not once, did any of the men send her a note. Zack had a sweet sentimental side to him. It was probably a reaction to the tough and gritty world he experienced at work.

Touched by Zack's romantic gesture, Lilli hurried into the ladies' room. Anxious as she was to read the note, she held back. She set the envelope on the counter, propped it against a romantic bouquet of red roses in a silver-trimmed vase. She liked to prolong good things, enjoying the exhilaration that came with anticipation.

Glancing at the envelope, she slipped off her blouse and dried herself with one of the monogrammed towels from the wicker basket next to the sink. She reapplied her makeup, brushed her hair, and slipped into Zack's jacket. She eyed the envelope and wondered what Zack's message said. Was he asking for a date? Her address and telephone number? Staring at the envelope, she felt like a kid in a fancy restaurant, eyeing the dessert tray's chocolate delights and whipped-cream fantasies while she worked her way through the appetizer, salad, and entree, knowing that the best was yet to come.

Unable to resist any longer, Lilli reached for the envelope. Slowly, savoring each moment, she pulled out the single sheet of folded paper and opened it. It wasn't Zack's handwriting. The block-print message, written in pencil, jumped off the page:

LEAVE GRAYROCKS NOW BEFORE IT'S TOO
LATE. SHOW THIS TO ANYONE AND YOU'RE
A DEAD WOMAN.

The letter and envelope fell from Lilli's trembling fingers. A small card slid out and landed on the floor. Lilli
leaned down and picked it up. She couldn't believe her
eyes. It was her business card. The one on which Bud
Conklin had scrawled 'Baywatch Inn.' The residue of tape
where Bud had affixed the card to his cash register was
visible.

Lilli shuddered. She whirled around to see if she was
being watched. Something rattled against the window near
the sink. She nearly jumped out of her skin. She quickly
stuffed the note and card into the envelope and shoved it
into the pocket of Zack's jacket, and hurried from the
bathroom.

She found the hostess near the front door. "Where is
the man who gave you this note?" She tried to sound
calm, but she could hear the nervousness in her voice.

"Oh, he's long gone."

"What did he look like?"

The hostess smiled. "A mystery man. He was wearing
dark glasses, black jeans, and a black tee shirt."

"Did he have dark hair?"

"I'm not sure. He was wearing a baseball cap. The
Yankees."

"Please, this is important."

"I can't say for sure," the hostess said. "It's dark in
here. I was busy. I'm sorry, but I didn't pay that much
attention." As Lilli turned to leave, the hostess said, "This
may not be important, but the man asked me to wait at
least fifteen minutes before handing you the note. And he
insisted that I give it to you when you were alone."

"Thanks," Lilli said. "I appreciate your help."

"If you don't mind me saying so," the hostess said. "You seem to have your share of interesting men." She nodded toward the rear of the room where Zack was waiting. "If you decide to give up the hunk in the back booth, let me know."

Lilli slid into the seat across from Zack and took a deep breath. "I'm glad you're still here," she said.

He leaned across the table toward her. "Are you always this insecure on a first date?"

"Don't say anything," she whispered. "Just reach under the table and put your hand on my knee."

"My mother never told me there would be days like this." He smiled. "Does it matter which knee?"

"This is serious," she said.

"I'll take that to mean either knee."

"I'm going to put something into your hand," she said.

"This is getting better by the minute."

"It's an envelope. With a note inside. I thought it was from you."

"Let me guess," he said. "It's from another man."

"Yes."

"So, now I'm involved in a rivalry for your affection. No problem. I like a challenging woman."

"Zack, just put your hand on my knee and take the envelope. Slide it onto the seat next to you, open it, and read it. Whatever you do, don't set it out where someone can see it."

"Lilli, it's dark in here. Haven't you noticed? No one can see anything."

"Just go along with me. After you read the note, you'll understand. You're a detective."

"You are serious," he said. His hand grazed her knee. He squeezed it gently. "Ready for the message," he said and she placed the envelope in his hand. "Message received," he said and turned nonchalantly toward the wall.

"And be careful," Lilli said, "my business card is in the envelope, too."

"A new marketing technique?" Zack asked. "Okay, okay," he said, "I'm opening the envelope."

Lilli watched Zack intently, waiting for the words to hit him. His jaw dropped. He turned toward her. "We need to contact the local police. This creep has threatened your life. We'll leave here immediately and get you back to Gram's. You'll be safer there than here."

"If we leave right away, and that guy is out there, he'll know I showed you the note. Maybe we should stay."

"Don't get me wrong. I'd like to stay here with you, but this is the wrong place and time." He signaled the waitress for the bill. "We're going to Baywatch Inn and we're calling the Grayrocks police. Gram can help us through the landmines of small-town protocol."

"There's one other thing," Lilli said. "He asked the hostess to wait fifteen minutes before giving me the envelope. What—?"

"He's buying time. He's setting up something. Come on. Hurry!"

He paid the check and steered Lilli to the front door.

Lilli asked, "Should we call the police and have them meet us here?"

"I don't think we should delay another minute." Zack glanced across the dimly lit parking lot. "We're going to move fast from here on in," he said. "Get in your Bronco, lock the doors, and drive to Gram's. I'll follow. Stay in your car until I get there." He checked the back seat. "Okay, let's go."

"What if he comes after us?"

"Car chase one-o-one. Don't worry. I'll run him off the

road. You just keep going. Don't stop for anyone or any-thing."

"You make it all sound so routine and simple." Then she noticed the worry lines between his eyes and the ten-sion in his jaw. "I'm glad you're here," she said. "I'll make this up to you."

"Promise?" he asked and she felt herself blush.

During the twenty-minute trip to Baywatch Inn, Lilli kept glancing from the rearview mirror to the road ahead. Her hands gripped the wheel. Zack followed closely. He was easy to spot in the green Miata convertible. No one tried to cut between them. Several cars approached in the opposite lane, but no one veered toward her or Zack or tried anything suspicious.

Each mile that brought Lilli closer to Gram's stirred up a jumble of thoughts. She tried to sort out the facts from the suppositions. The man had taken her camera and ex-posed a roll of film. He had tried to run her off the road. He had threatened her life. He had been seen talking to Betty and Clarissa Morgan. He had bought a Polaroid camera at Bud Conklin's Camera Shoppe. He had some-how gotten hold of stationery from Baywatch Inn and her business card from Bud's shop.

How did all these puzzle pieces fit together? She didn't know, but one thing was certain. She wasn't going back to New York City and leave her photo assignment unfin-ished. She only had a few days and then she would be done. She would stick it out. She would remain calm, but aware of danger. The police would do their job. Zack could be counted on in an emergency. And so could Gram.

That's when it struck her. This wasn't the first time trouble had come to Grayrocks. Gram's granddaughter, Annie, and Annie's husband, Matt, had been injured, their lives threatened. And Annie's parents, Gram's daughter and son-in-law, had been murdered. Did Gram mention if the murderer had been caught? Was there any possible connection between those incidents and what was happening now? The more she thought, the more confused she became. The puzzle was growing larger, the pieces more scattered.

Lilli approached Baywatch Inn. As she turned into the driveway that led to the parking lot, she noticed a police car parked in the street. She looked in the rear view mirror. Zack was right behind her. Why would the police be here? Had Zack called from his car? Had the Morgans been located?

Seconds later, Zack pulled in next to her. "The police are already here. Something's happened." Concern crossed his handsome face. "Are you okay?"

"Yes," she said. "No one's going to drive me away until I've finished my work assignment. Right now, I'm concerned about the Morgans. You don't think something's happened to them, do you?"

"Come on," he said, taking her hand. They hurried along the path toward the front of the inn. He opened the door and looked inside. The lobby was deserted.

"Gram?" Zack called out.

A squeaking noise came from behind them.

"What was that?" Lilli said, nearly jumping out of her skin.

"Who's there?" Zack said, shielding Lilli.

"It's me," Gram said. "Who'd you expect, a ghost?" The rocking chair squeaked as Gram stood up. She came forward from the darkness, the glow of the porch light reflected off her glasses. "I didn't want to be at the door in case you two planned on something more than just a simple good-night kiss."

Zack shook his head. "You are such a romantic."

"And hungry for sweet revenge." Gram squared her shoulders. "I called the police station. Hank, he's the chief of police, insisted on coming himself. He could have sent one of his Boys in Blue. This isn't exactly the crime of the century."

"What happened?" Lilli asked.

"I was in my office, looking through my toolbox, deciding which wrench would fix the pipe under the kitchen sink. Nobody was in the lobby when I left, but suddenly I heard noises, like keys rattling, coming from the reception counter. I gripped a wrench in each hand and peeked out. Some man was messing with my keys and rifling through my registration book. 'What do you want?' I asked. I startled him. By now I was next to him. He pushed past me and knocked me aside, saying 'Out of my way, old woman.' If he could fight dirty like that, so could I."

Gram wound her arm around like a pitcher ready to unleash a fastball. "I flung my wrench at him. Caught him square in the back, right between the shoulder blades. You should have heard him yowl! I let fly the second wrench and nailed his skinny butt." Gram snorted, stifling a laugh. "He flew out of here, like hornets were chasing him."

"Are you okay?" Lilli asked.

"Of course," Gram replied. "It takes more than a push and a shove to keep me down."

"You're one tough woman," Zack said, patting her shoulder.

"Have the Morgans returned yet?" Lilli asked.

"No, but Mr. Morgan insists that everything is under control. Hank has been talking to him, says he'll give that matter another day and then he'll pull Morgan in for some official questioning. Hank was salivating at the very thought."

"Had the man gotten upstairs to any of the guest rooms?" Zack asked.

"No," Gram said. "I'd been at the reception counter all evening. I would have seen him. But I'll bet he was headed upstairs, to steal what he could."

"How long ago did this happen?" Zack asked.

Gram checked her watch. "About a half hour ago."

Lilli figured the mystery man had enough time to leave her the note and get back to Baywatch Inn. With the time she had spent in the rest room, with the hostess, and talking to Zack, the man had plenty of lead-time.

Zack must have been reading her mind. "It could be him," he said. "He had enough time."

"Could you identify the man?" Zack asked.

"Not really," Gram said.

"Could it be the man Annie sketched?" Lilli asked.

"Maybe. I don't know," Gram flustered. "It all happened so fast. He came and went, all in a matter of seconds." She chuckled. "If he dares to go swimming, you'll find him. He'll be the guy with a welt in the middle of his back. Check out his rear end. There will be a welt there too."

Chapter Seven

Hank

"Hank Borden, meet Lilli and Zack." Gram hooked her arm around Hank's pudgy waist and steered him from the stairs toward Lilli and Zack. Puffing out his chest, Hank hiked up his belt and holster. He struck a pose beneath the twinkle lights draped above the reception alcove. His badge, centered on the pocket of his starched blue uniform shirt, glinted. His black shoes shone as if he'd spit and polished them for hours. Lilli noticed the extra thickness of his soles and heels, which added about two inches to his height and made him slightly taller than Gram.

"Like I was telling you," Gram said, "Lilli Masters's photographs are going to put Grayrocks on the map. And this handsome lug is, well, he's calling himself Zack Faraday. He's in town for a wedding."

Everyone shook hands. Hank exuded self-importance as he strode to the door and tested the locks. "As a precaution," he said to Gram, "keep your doors locked tonight." He checked the latches on the two long narrow windows that framed the door. "Lock those windows, too." Lilli thought he looked like a bird that didn't dare land for fear the larger birds would peck him to pieces.

Gram turned to Zack and Lilli. "Hank and I go way back."

Hank smiled and the toothpick clenched between his front teeth slid to the corner of his mouth. "Way back to Grayrocks Elementary. We sat next to each other in kindergarten. My crush on her lasted until eighth grade."

Gram turned up her nose. "That's when those two new girls came to town. They thought they were hot stuff."

"They were," Hank ventured. Gram shot him a glance loaded with daggers. Hank closed his mouth and chomped on the toothpick. "Well, now, let's forget the past and talk about my official investigation right here at your inn."

"What did you discover?" Gram said.

Hank shifted foot to foot. "I've discovered that lots of people have been touching your banister, reception desk, and registration book. It won't be easy isolating fingerprints. I asked around and none of your guests saw or heard anything. So—" He drew the toothpick from his mouth and twirled it between his stubby fingers. "We only have your word for the attempted theft of the keys and registration book."

Gram flustered. "Since when isn't my word good enough?"

"Hold onto your sails," Hank said. "I'm just playing the devil's advocate. That's how they do it on 'Law and Order.' I'm saying what any lawyer worth his salt would say. Without eyewitnesses and missing items, there's not much of a case. As far as I can tell—" His arms sprung away from his sides like the wings of a bird learning to fly. "Criminal activity may have been interrupted, but no crime took place."

Hank focused his beady eyes on Lilli. "I'm getting vibrations from you, Miss Lilli Masters. Do you have something to tell me or do you always huff and puff like that when an officer of the law is present?"

Lilli forced herself to remain calm. "I think the man who was rifling through Gram's stuff wanted to know which room I was staying in. He planned to take the key and get into my room. He wants to steal something from me, or scare me, or hurt me. This isn't my first encounter with him, if he's who I think he is."

"You know him?"

"Not exactly." Lilli pulled the envelope from her purse. "I have proof that someone, and I'm pretty sure it's the same man who was here, is after me. Zack's a New York City detective. He can back up what I say."

"New York City?" Hank slapped his forehead. "Here comes trouble nipping at my heels like a hungry dog!"

"Detective?" Gram smiled. "Why, Zack Faraday, you sneaky devil. You've been holding out on me. I'll bet you're here on a big case, preparing for your next role."

Zack shrugged, pretending exasperation. "I came here to relax and enjoy my cousin Tim's wedding. So far, it's been an interesting experience."

"Let's sit down," Gram said. "I'm tired from all the carpentry repairs I did today. And now all this news. I'm like my computer after a busy weekend—overloaded and ready to crash."

Everyone followed Gram into the lounge. It was crammed with chairs and couches, slip-covered with a beige cotton print that portrayed comical beach scenes. Several end tables, a huge oval coffee table, and racks overflowing with magazines filled the remaining spaces.

Lilli figured that the fireplace drew visitors to the room on chilly fall evenings. Gram plunked down on a couch. On the wall above her head hung maps of the world, the United States, New York State, and Long Island. Each was punctured with hundreds of colorful pins.

Gram tilted her head back and said, "I don't suppose he put a pin on the town he's from." She chuckled. "My guests love these maps, although the returning customers feel cheated. They want a special pin to indicate that they've been here twice or three times or—"

Hank cleared his throat.

"I'm sorry, Hank," Gram said, "I shouldn't be carrying on like this during your official investigation."

Hank pulled a notebook and pencil from his pocket and settled into the plump cushions next to Lilli. "Start at the beginning. Don't leave nothing out. I'll decide what's important." He wet the tip of his pencil and, with a flourish, placed it at the top of the page.

The words spilled from Lilli's mouth. The man had been seen near the fishing pier with the Morgan women. She suspected that he might have hurt them. He might have come to the inn not only to break into her room, but also the Morgans' room, to steal, or possibly to harm Mr. Morgan.

"Hold it," Hank said. "Gram filled me in about the Morgan women and the games Mrs. Morgan played. But, go on," he said.

Lilli picked up the story. Outside Conklin's Camera Shoppe, the man took her camera. Flora and Mary Lou Conklin had actually seen the man.

"Hold it," Hank said again. "Mary Lou Conklin? That puts a new wrinkle on this case. She's out for Gram's hide. She could be stirring up trouble, saying she saw him. Does she know you're staying here?"

Lilli nodded.

Hank jotted away furiously. "She could be trying to keep Gram busy here so she can have her daddy all to herself."

Gram said, "Hank, you're carrying this a bit too far. Mary Lou is possessive, but—"

Hank interrupted, "Shakespeare not withstanding, Hell hath no fury like a daughter pushed aside."

"It's possible Mary Lou was somehow involved," Lilli said. "The guy knew where I was staying because he had my business card. Bud Conklin had scribbled 'Baywatch Inn' on the back and then taped it to his cash register. Either the guy stole it or—"

Hank said, "Or Bud or Mary Lou Conklin gave it to him." He scribbled more notes. "Now, Lilli, where were we?"

Lilli picked up her storytelling about the gray truck that tried to run her off Soundshore Road. She realized that every time she expressed her feelings or elaborated with details Hank mumbled, "Uh-huh. Uh-huh. Uh-huh." Occasionally he asked, "What time was that?" or "Where exactly was that?" Lilli glanced at the pad each time he jotted something down. He limited his entries to names, times, and addresses.

She continued, promising herself to stick to the facts. The man had given the threatening note to the hostess at the Soundview Lodge to pass on to her. He had asked the hostess to delay giving her the note, possibly buying time to get to the inn before her. And now he had come to the inn, probably to get into her room. Lilli realized that possibilities and probabilities shaded almost every sentence. But her intuition had rarely tricked her in the past and she would rely on it now.

Lilli shuddered. "Maybe he planned to hide in my room

and kill me. That's what he threatened to do if I showed the note to anyone. Maybe he figured I showed it to Zack." Gram reached across the couch and patted Lilli's arm.

Lilli folded her hands and sat back. "That's it. That's everything I can think of."

"Thank you, Lilli. You'd make an excellent witness in a courtroom. A very dramatic presentation. Some of it useful, some of it fluff, if you don't mind my saying so." He held up his hand. "I know what you're thinking, that I'm not taking this whole matter seriously enough. You're wrong. The man who took your camera and ruined your film is guilty of disturbing the peace and destruction of personal property."

He pulled a slim plastic envelope from his pocket. He carefully slipped in the note, envelope, and Lilli's business card. "The man who gave you this note threatened you, there's no denying that, and the Grayrocks Police Department will not tolerate any threat. My only problem is, you're rolling so many different things into one big ball of wax. We don't know if one man did all these things. You didn't see the driver of the truck or the man who wrote this note. And Gram can't identify the intruder."

Lilli flustered, "But—"

"Let me have my say," Hank interrupted. "We'll start with concrete evidence. We have Annie's sketch and Flora the florist's eyewitness account. We'll start there. We'll find that man or both men, bring them in, and get an accounting of their whereabouts. We'll check out their alibis. That's police procedure, and that's how we do things here. By the book."

"But—"

"No buts about it." Hank snapped the pad shut and

placed it in his back pocket. "I'll have Pete, Charly, and Joe, that's my Boys in Blue, check out everything. They're good men. We'll find this guy who threatened you and get to the bottom of things."

"But—"

Hank wagged his finger, "Now Lilli, I'm not saying you have a wild imagination or a journalist's sense of padding the facts to make up a good story. If anything else happens that makes you feel threatened, let me assure you, we have a safe house right here in Grayrocks."

Zack leaned forward in his chair. "I wouldn't have figured on a safe house in a town of this size."

Hank smiled. "It's my own home. And there's no safer place anywhere in the world. My wife, folks around here call her the Warden, wouldn't allow anyone to set foot in our house unless she gave the okay. And, trust me, no one slips past my Lizzie." He shook his head and chuckled. "Lizzie has bionic ears, x-ray vision, a bloodhound's nose, and eyes in the back of her head. Yes, sir, she's got it all. Course, that's not always a good thing. Fact is, she robbed me of my poker night. She said she couldn't sleep as long as I was out. I couldn't stay out knowing she was tossing and turning. She's what you might call 'devoted.' "

Gram chuckled. "Come on, Hank. Tell Lilli and Zack the real reason people stay away from your house."

"It's my wife's name," Hank said. His face beamed with pride. "Lizzie Jones, that's her given name. Then she married me, Hank Borden. Now she's Lizzie Borden!"

Lilli gulped and Zack laughed heartily.

Hank continued, "Folks picture my Lizzie gripping an axe in both hands, her arms raised ready to strike. The joke around the station house is, if there's ever a murder investigation, I should take Lizzie along. 'Just introduce her to the suspects' the Boys in Blue say, 'and any murderer will run for his life.' The Boys love her, just like I do, and they have fun teasing her. It was their idea to call my place a safe house. So far, I've never had to use it. But the offer stands, any time."

Zack said, "If you and the Boys in Blue would like some extra help with this problem, count me in."

Hank's lip curled. "My Boys and I can handle this problem."

"I'm sure you can," Zack said cordially. "You run a nice tight ship here and—"

"I know when somebody's sweet talking me," Hank snapped. "And right now, Zack, honey is flowing from your lips. The floor is getting sticky from it."

"I didn't mean—"

"You made your point." Hank huffed. "You don't think me and the Boys can handle any trouble brewing here. You think only New York City cops know what's what. Well, you're wrong. Dead wrong. We're every bit as good as you guys, and maybe better when it comes to spotting what makes people tick. Take Mr. Morgan, for instance. He's hurting. His wife's making him squirm. She wants some extra loving to make up for the missing daughter. See? We get it. We understand the heart, the mind, the soul, the whole nine yards."

"I'm impressed," Zack said.

"I hear that attitude coming through loud and clear, Mister. You're pushing me against the wall. You think I'll say some cornball small-town hokey thing like, 'This town ain't big enough for the two of us.' But let me hit the nail, square on the head. You don't have any jurisdiction in Grayrocks and if you get in my way, I'll have your butt whipped. Do I make myself clear?"

"Just one thing is fuzzy," Zack said. "Who is doing this butt-whipping? You or the Boys in Blue?"

Hank's toothpick jumped up and down between his teeth. "The pleasure will be all mine." He spit out the words like bullets.

Zack reached forward and pumped Hank's hand as if he expected water to flow. "You've got style, Hank. I don't blame you for resenting city slickers invading your territory, pushing their urban techniques down your throat. But for the record, I'm a country boy."

Hank cocked his head to one side. "What are you saying?"

"I grew up in Goshen. It's about the size of Grayrocks. You and me, we're small-town guys. We have to stick together."

"I gotta hear this," Hank scoffed.

Zack said, "The city folks are buying up the farmland in Goshen and clogging the country lanes with their fancy cars. They beep at tractors crossing the road, yelling for them to get out of the way. You're lucky. You're three hours from New York City. Goshen's only an hour. You get visitors. Goshen gets—" Zack's eyes glinted. "Goshen gets commuters."

Hank stroked his chin. "So you're a farm boy, eh?"

"Corn. My dad and uncles grow corn. Faraday corn-fed all the tourists who came to the big resorts in nearby Sullivan County."

"Okay, I have a slightly different picture of you now."

Zack laughed. "Hayseed coming out of my ears?"

"Something like that," Hank said. He squinted. "But my warning still holds tight. Don't get in my way. Don't hamper my investigation."

"No problem," Zack said. "You've got professional written all over you. Let me amend my offer. I'm here to dance at my cousin's wedding. If you can find a better way for me to utilize my time, you know where to find me. I'll be at the church, the reception, or the Anchorage Inn. That's where I'm staying."

"You poor thing," Gram said and pursed her lips. "That's such a fussy place. They've got a snooty French chef. He calls fries 'freeeetz' and chicken is 'poo-lay.' Now who in their right mind would taste anything with a name like that? He must be nuts, or 'fooo,' as they say in Pa-ree. And desserts? He never heard of pie. All he knows are frou-frou pastries and—"

Hank held up his hand. "Thanks for the gastronomical survey, Gram, but I think it's time to get back to the investigation." He turned toward Zack, a smile creeping across his face. "Is that how it's done in New York City, or do you let every conversation run its course?"

Zack said, "We keep the train on the tracks, the same as you. Oh, I'm sorry. You probably say 'we keep the boat between the buoys.' Am I right?"

Hank said, "In case you haven't noticed, we have trains as well as boats here in Grayrocks."

Zack said, "Good point. I'll try to be more observant."

"You can learn a lot from me," Hank said, "but I think you've already figured that out. Now Lilli, how about bringing me that camera? We'll see if the guy left a set of fingerprints on it or the note. With the Labor Day holiday, it might take some extra time, but we'll get on it as soon as possible. And while you're at it, let's have a look at your photographs." He turned to Zack. "Here in Grayrocks, we leave no stone unturned."

Zack quipped, "That's a big job, considering all the rocky beaches around here."

Gram said, "I'm glad you two are keeping your sense of humor. For a minute there, I thought you would rip each other's throats out. Then who would I call? The police? You bozos are the police. What a crazy world!"

Lilli returned a few minutes later with the camera and photographs. "I don't see anything incriminating in the photos," she said fanning them across the coffee table. "There are no shots of him or anyone who resembles him. I don't get it."

"Neither do I," Hank said. "It could be a wild goose chase." He passed the photos, one by one, to Zack, Gram, and Lilli. "Fine work here, Lilli," he said when he'd seen them all. "I agree with Gram, your photos could help business here in Grayrocks."

Hank stroked his chin. "Tell you what, my Boys in Blue will be busy this weekend with traffic situations, tempers flaring and so on. But I'm going to tell them to keep their eyes peeled for the Morgan women and the guy in the sketch. I'll have a few dozen copies made up. What's more, we'll watch Mr. Morgan's every move and we'll keep an eye out for any strange happenings here at Baywatch Inn."

Hank stood up and headed toward the door. "And, of course, they'll be keeping their eyes on you, Lilli." He chuckled. "They'll take their cue from this ole country boy, Zack."

Chapter Eight

The Jetty

Gram leaned across the porch railing. "Be careful, Lilli," she said.

"You, too," Lilli replied.

"We'll both be fine. One of the Boys in Blue will cruise by here every hour and the beach crowd will keep their eyes on you." Gram smiled. "I tucked some surprises into your tote bag."

Lilli peeked. "Blueberry muffins and some bottled water. Thanks."

"I prefer well water," Gram said. "But you have to roll with the times. I've come to accept sun-dried tomatoes and microwave popcorn. Guess I can abide by bottled water."

Gram waved goodbye and Lilli noticed gauze strips tied around the index finger of Gram's left hand. "What happened to your finger?"

"I hit myself with the hammer. My carpentry skills are a bit rusty."

"Good thing you weren't using a saw," Lilli said and waved goodbye. As she walked down the path, she thought, Mary Lou Conklin said the man in the sketch was missing part of his index finger. Could he be a carpenter? He had a farmer's tan. Carpenters often worked outdoors, especially since so many houses on this part of Long Island had porches.

Lilli turned back to mention it to Gram, but Gram had already gone inside. She would tell Hank. Not that Hank would consider it an important piece of information. He would call it another piece of fluff. Another bit of string in her big ball of wax.

Lilli tucked her long-sleeved denim shirt into her jeans. She wiggled her toes in Annie's beat-up thick-soled sneakers that Gram had insisted she wear. She checked her tote to make sure she had Gram's work gloves. She would be well protected from the jetty's sharp rocks and barnacles.

The sun was just peeking over the roofs of the tourist inns as Lilli turned onto the street and set out for Grayrocks Beach. Only a few people were moving about. Two boys strolled along, carrying fishing poles and buckets of chum. A girl in a bathing suit pedaled her bike. A man with stooped shoulders, his face wizened from years of sunlight reflecting off water, swept away grass clippings that littered the path to his inn.

Curtains ruffled through the open windows of houses. Smart tourists were sleeping late, Lilli thought, enjoying the cool morning breezes. Church bells rang out and echoed through the street. Grayrocks was such a pretty peaceful town. Maybe she was wrong and Hank was right. Her imagination often ran wild and she did dramatize events.

But then she remembered her fear when she had nearly been run off the road and when she had read the threatening note. A chill ran up her spine. Grayrocks was pretty, almost idyllic, but danger lurked on busy streets, on deserted roads, and even at Gram's inn. She would get on with her work, but she would be careful. She would depend on instinct and intuition to guide her every step.

When Lilli arrived at the beach, she was surprised to find a small crowd, mostly kids, swimming. Most of the adults sat on blankets, nibbling muffins and sipping steaming cups of coffee from oversized thermoses. And it was only eight-thirty in the morning! Her curiosity got the better of her. She walked toward a young couple. "Would you mind if I took some pictures?" she asked. "I'm with *Viewpoint* magazine."

"We know who you are," the man said. "You're Lilli Masters. Gram called us last night and asked us to spread the word. She told us we'd be seeing a pretty redhead at the beach and all over town toting an arsenal of cameras. She said you'd be good for business. We like to hear that. She told us about the trouble. Just put that clear out of your head. We'll be keeping an eye on you. Gram threatened to cut off her supply of blueberry pie if anyone harmed a hair on your head."

The pretty brunette stood up, shaking the sand off her shorts. "I'm Patty Kramkowski. And this is my husband Steve. And all these folks . . . Hellooooo!" she called out and people in the water and on the shore waved and called out cheery greetings. "They'd like to meet you, but they're not going to rush over and make a big fuss over you. Gram's instructions were to let you get your job done. We appreciate any help you can give our local businesses."

Steve, a gangly man with a shock of blond hair, rose

to his knees. Balancing his coffee mug in one hand and a muffin in the other, he pointed beyond the parking lot. "We run that towel shop on the corner."

"I saw your towels at Baywatch Inn," Lilli said. "I liked the one with the surf whipping toward the tourists and their arms are raised like the Statue of Liberty's."

"That's the Big Wave from Grayrocks." Steve laughed. "Tourists love them. They haven't noticed that the surf never gets that high or rough."

Patty said, "They don't notice much of anything. It's like they take long-lasting shots of novocaine before they arrive in Grayrocks. And they follow up with booster shots every time reality starts to set it."

Steve chimed in, "Patty says they've got a bad case of vacation-itis." He smiled. "And Patty's always right. The towel idea was hers."

"It's very cute," Lilli said. "I'll take a picture of your store later and I'll be sure to include the towel."

Steve said, "We take a few hours off every Sunday morning and come here."

"Anyone here at this hour is a local," Patty said. "The churches put on early-morning services so we can pray for business and then open up on time."

Steve gulped the last of his coffee. "While the tourists sleep, we take back our beaches. It's our local style of activism."

Lilli enjoyed Steve and Patty's easy-going bantering. She sensed that they complained about the tourists but, deep down, they enjoyed them, and realized their livelihood depended on them. "I'll leave you alone now and get to work," Lilli said.

She snapped photos of the people on the beach enjoying family time. There were no sand-castle competitions, horseshoe contests, or volleyball games, just local people spending a pleasant hour or two, replenishing themselves before the next onslaught of tourists.

Lilli soon turned her attention to the kids in the water. Many floated around in old inner tubes. No touristy water wings or fancy floats shaped like sharks for them. Some, wearing masks and fins, plunged down, and seconds later, broke through the surface of the water, waving a handful of shells. One kid, with his wet hair pasted onto his forehead, called out, "It's sharp. I think it's an arrowhead."

Steve and Patty strolled past Lilli. "We'll be leaving and wanted to say goodbye," Patty said. Steve shielded his eyes and nodded toward the water, "See that girl with the yellow mask? She's searching for arrowheads."

"Montauk arrowheads, I'll bet," Lilli said. "Gram told me this is an old Montauk Indian area."

Patty added, "None of us paid much attention to Indian things until Matt Revington came to town and married Gram's granddaughter, Annie. Matt's part Montauk and Annie's making a name for herself with her Montauk paintings." She shifted her beach bag onto her shoulder. "Thanks to them, we're a lot more aware of the Indian contribution to our country."

Steve tugged down his Grayrocks High School baseball cap. "Matt's trying to rev up interest in restoring Montauk ceremonial places here in Grayrocks." He pointed toward the jetty. "He wants the town council to set aside funds to preserve the Montauk Steps."

"Gram told me to keep an eye out for the Steps." Lilli shielded her eyes. "Where are they?"

"It's a pathway of big stone platforms. They descend from Bay Street down to Clam Hollow, over there beyond the jetty." Steve pointed again. "You can't see them from here. The trees block your view, but there are thirteen platforms."

Patty added, "One for each tribe in the Montauk Confederation. Matt says each chief stood on a step before they began their pow-wows."

"It showed a kind of pecking order," Steve said. "The oldest chief, or the one with the most people, or the most whale tails, whatever, stood at the top." He nudged Lilli. "What a great picture that would have made. The Montauk chiefs with all their feathers and fancy wampum jewelry."

"You've got my curiosity up," Lilli said. "I think I'll take a look at those Montauk Steps."

"Be careful," Patty warned. "The Steps are roped off on Bay Street to keep people away until guard rails are built. And going over the jetty to get to the Steps is too difficult. Until the town council springs into action—and that could take years—there's no easy way to get to them. There are pictures in the library. That's your best bet."

"Thanks. I'll follow up on that." Lilli sensed the couple's pride in their unique past. She was very happy that she had come to the beach so early on a Sunday morning. She felt refreshed, revitalized, and inspired. Photos of the locals at the height of the season, escaping the hurly-burly and enjoying the natural resources would make a great feature in her story. Thinking aloud, she said, "I'm going to ask *Viewpoint*'s editors if they would consider an additional article on the Montauk influence on Grayrocks and surrounding areas. I'll try to meet Matt Revington and approach him about it."

Patty tapped her watch. "Like clockwork," she said. "It's nine-thirty and here come the tourists. Gram wanted me to remind you, don't go anywhere alone."

"Don't worry," Lilli said, scanning the parking lot. She looked for a beat-up pickup truck, its pale gray paint oxidized and powdery looking. But there was no truck in sight. She watched the tourists arrive and the locals depart. It was like the changing of the guard at Buckingham Palace.

Lilli captured Patty and Steve waving goodbye and figured she could work it in with their towel items. Soon, all the locals were gone and the beach became more colorful, more noisy, more crowded.

Lilli continued snapping away. She realized how easy it was to tell the tourists from the locals. The tourists carted armloads of paraphernalia. Their skin was sunburned, although they wore really goofy hats and gobs of white and very shiny clownish-looking sunscreen. A photographer's dream come true.

At ten o'clock Lilli recorded her reactions into her tape recorder and gathered up her belongings. She walked toward the jetty and noticed a half-dozen DANGER RIP TIDE signs posted along the way. At the jetty, she pulled on Gram's work gloves. A trace of blood on the glove's index finger of the left hand caught her attention. She reminded herself to tell Hank about the man missing part of his finger. It could be important in identifying him, especially where fingerprints were involved.

She began inching her way over the slippery stones of the jetty. The seaweed and barnacles slowed her down.

Stopping for a moment to tie her sneakers, she looked toward the abandoned brick building. Nothing red appeared near it. Her gaze wandered to the thick grove of trees on the far embankment that ran parallel to the jetty. She pulled her field glasses from her tote. Peering through them, she noticed a rusty wire fence winding through the trees. There were more signs. NO TRESPASSING. DANGER. KEEP OUT. She was putting her field glasses into her tote when she heard someone calling her name.

She looked over her shoulder. "Zack?" She teetered on

the top of the jetty and looked down at Zack standing on the beach.

"Gram said you'd be here. One of the tourists saw you come this way."

Lilli thought Zack looked incredibly handsome in his dark suit. "The latest gear for strolling the beach?" she asked.

"For the wedding," he said. "That's why I'm here. I need you."

Lilli blushed. She didn't know what to say.

Zack rushed on, "Actually it's my cousin who needs you. To photograph the wedding. The photographer is a family friend of the bride's from Riverhead. He broke his leg and right now he's in the hospital emergency room. He'll come along when he can, but there's no telling how late or mobile he'll be. The wedding is at noon, but they want the usual pictures beforehand. I know that you're busy with your own work, but could you possibly help out?"

"Sure. I'm glad to return a favor."

"For what?"

"For escorting me from the Soundshore Lodge."

"Aw shucks, ma'am, it was nothing." He flashed his lopsided grin. "Damsels in distress are my specialty."

She inched back over the jetty. "Don't come too close," she said. "You'll get ripped to pieces."

"Usually women don't give advance warnings," he said. "I appreciate it."

Lilli was too busy climbing and skidding along on her butt to reply. Finally, with a few feet to go, she handed Zack her tote and jumped down onto the sand.

"I need to change," she said, pulling off her gloves.

Zack checked his watch. "Can you be ready in, uh, ten

minutes? I realize these are not the words most women want to hear."

"Deadlines," Lilli huffed. "My life is a series of deadlines. The good news is, I don't need to pore through an extensive wardrobe. I have only one dress with me. So, okay, give me ten minutes."

When they entered the Baywatch lobby, Gram rushed toward them. "Is everything okay?"

"Yes," Lilli said. "I'm off to the wedding with Zack."

Gram studied Zack from head to toe. "You look very presidential, just the way you did in *Air Force One*. Do those Hollywood producers let you keep the wardrobe?"

Lilli dropped her damp clothes in a heap and quickly washed up. She unrolled her little black dress, actually a long clingy tee shirt, and slipped it over her head. It slithered down her body and swung to a halt mid-calf. She smoothed the fabric over her slim hips and thanked her photography professor for the advice, "On any assignment, even in the jungle, take along a black dress." The jungle. *Raiders of the Lost Ark*. Harrison Ford running for his life through the jungle, swinging on a rope over crocodile-infested water, into a seaplane. Such craziness! She was carrying on worse than Gram. His name is Zack Faraday and he's a detective, she reminded herself, tugging on her black sandals. A very handsome detective.

Then she looked in the mirror and cringed. She grabbed hold of her hair with both hands, twisted it, tamed it, and pinned it up with a rhinestone clip. Curls sprung free, framing her face. She ran a tube of tawny-apricot gloss across her lips and dabbed blusher on her cheeks. She hurried down the stairs, her tote bag slapping against her leg.

"Wow!" Zack said. "Just think what you could have done with another ten minutes."

"Men!" Lilli muttered as she passed by Gram.

"Snags," Gram said.

"Snags?" Lilli asked.

"S-N-A-G-S. Sensitive New-Age Guys," Gram said and laughed.

Chapter Nine

The Wedding

"This area is reserved for the wedding party," Zack said, pulling the Miata between the white streamers.

Lilli stepped out of his car and stopped to admire the surroundings. She liked the sense of privacy offered by the forsythia and lilac hedges. Although no longer in bloom, they separated the parking lot from the street.

"This way," Zack said, lugging her tote and gripping her elbow firmly, as if she might change her mind and run off. He steered her toward the gray clapboard church hall, its white trim glistening in the sunshine. Flowerbeds, mulched with oyster shells, encircled the hall. White painted benches, made of oars supported by anchors, added nautical touches to the country charm.

"They're expecting you," Zack said, hurrying up the porch steps, "but I'd better brief you on the situation first." He leaned against the porch railing. "They're getting dressed. Tim said it's a madhouse. The zipper on the maid of honor's dress got stuck. One bouquet arrived wilted. A bridesmaid couldn't find the matching bracelet she was supposed to wear. The bride's mother is crying. Margie, that's the bride, can't stop fine-tuning the last-minute details."

"Maybe we should wait for the wedding photographer."

"Oh no. You're just what they need, a fresh perspective. But let me give you the rest of it. The groom's mother, that's my Aunt Trudy, is bossing everybody around, including the wedding coordinator. You can't miss the coordinator. She's the one with the purple hat." Zack stretched out his arms, beyond his shoulders, his palms facing each other. "A really big hat. When I left, she was threatening to wrestle Aunt Trudy to the ground if she didn't stay out of the way."

Zack handed Lilli her tote bag and nudged her gently toward the doorway. "Good luck. You'll need it." He cocked his eyebrow, smiled his lopsided smile, and said, "Remember, they're counting on you to provide memories that will last a lifetime."

Lilli walked into the hall with the enthusiasm of someone about to face a firing squad.

"Thanks for coming," exclaimed the fiery-eyed bride, who rushed from the dressing room, notepad and pen in hand, exuberance bursting from her like fireworks on the Fourth of July. Her gown billowed around her. Her veil cascaded away from the cluster of curls perched on the top of her head like yellow petals. "I'm Margie Schyler. You're a life saver, Lilli," she said, shaking hands. "I'll be in your debt forever."

Margie pulled out her notepad and ticked off an item. "It's ugly in the dressing room right now. I told them they have five minutes to shape up and then you're coming in, cameras blazing, capturing their true personalities on film for all eternity." She glanced at her notepad. "Before we go in, I'd like you to meet Arabelle Revington. Arabelle's agreed to help you in any way possible. She knows everyone. She'll give you the inside scoop and smooth over any problems."

"Arabelle Revington?" Lilli asked. "Isn't she Matt Revington's aunt?"

Margie nodded. "She's also my friend and employer." She checked her watch. "We better give the bridesmaids another two minutes in the dressing room. You know Gram, right? Well, she recommended me to Arabelle to help out after David, her husband, died. Arabelle was lost without him. She needed someone to help with the calls and correspondence and things. I'm very detail-oriented, so Arabelle kept me on, a combination personal assistant and house manager." Margie gulped in a breath and charged on. "A lucky break for someone my age. I oversee the gardeners, cook, chauffeur, and other staff at her estate in East Bay."

"A very responsible job," Lilli commented, awed by Margie's rapid-fire delivery. "And a lovely setting, from what I hear."

"East Bay is beautiful, but it's so quiet you can hear the grass grow. Arabelle lives in one of those secluded homes, mansions actually, east of Grayrocks, at the very tip of Long Island. It's too depressing for Arabelle. As Gram has probably told you, Arabelle can be very reclusive. She hardly ever left home even before David died. She has some kind of nervous disorder, requiring trips to European clinics and all, but Annie and I make sure she gets out and meets some real down-home people, not just those stuffed-shirts in the country-club set. Arabelle is finally learning to loosen up. As they say on 'Oprah,' she's letting her feelings hang out to dry."

Lilli couldn't believe all Margie's chattering away and on the most important day of her life.

Margie took another deep breath. "Gram deserves some credit for the 'new' Arabelle. She's even convinced Arabelle to take up bicycling. Stanley, that's Arabelle's chauffeur, hides her bike in the trunk of her car and spirits them off to Gram's, where he drags the bike out, polishes it, dusts off the seat, tests the bell, and fills the basket with picnic goodies. Then off she pedals with Gram. What a sight! She wears a disguise of sorts, something like a beekeeper's get-up with a veiled hat, and pretends nobody knows who she is. Everybody knows! She comes back home from those outings bubbling over with stories. Worse than me, even. Sorry. Here I am blabbing away, delaying the photographs of my own wedding. Oh, good. Here's Arabelle."

Margie checked her watch. "I'll let you two get acquainted. There must be something I didn't tell you about her. And, of course, I didn't know what to tell her about you, except what Tim heard from Zack. Whew! Your ears must be ringing!"

"I'd like to hear—"

Margie interrupted, "Give me two minutes to get everybody's head on straight and then come in. Feel free to ignore the wedding coordinator. My mother insisted on hiring her, to add a touch of class, she said. A woman in her bingo group suggested her. Bunny Wallingham is her name. I don't need her, but I didn't want to hurt my mother's feelings. My mother is very temperamental. But that's buckets of teardrops over the dam, as they say on 'Oprah.' Lilli, thanks oodles. Did I say that before? Oops, then thanks again. Oodles and oodles!" She was still talking as she flew into the dressing room in a cloud of white organza and the door closed behind her. Lilli felt breathless and she had barely said a word.

"You must be Lilli," said the petite, elegant woman, coming down the hallway and extending her hand. She was immaculately dressed in a jade-green silk suit that accentuated her dark curly hair and creamy skin. "I'm Arabelle Revington."

Lilli shook hands and said, "I hear very nice things about your nephew, Matt, and his talented wife, Annie. Much of what I've heard comes from Gram Jenkins. She insists she's not biased."

"Every word she said is true." Arabelle flashed her brilliant smile. "Matt is a great guy and Annie is very special to me. Her mother, Caitlin, and I were friends. Annie fills some of the void left by Caitlin's passing. Caitlin taught me, or should I say, tried to teach me some photography skills. Annie tried too. I'm frightfully awful. But eventually something has to rub off, don't you think? I'll be watching your techniques. Rest assured, however, that I'll stay out of your way, unless you need me. Bunny will be at your elbow, anticipating your every move, and orchestrating those you hadn't even considered."

"I'm sure you'll be helpful. Shall we get started?" Lilli liked Arabelle immediately. She was an odd blend of well-bred reserve and cheery straightforwardness.

"Into the war zone," Arabelle said and turned the dressing room doorknob. "Let me warn you," she said as the door swung open, "the first landmine is an eye-popping vision in purple."

No sooner had the word 'purple' been uttered, than a tall, angular woman, her silver hair teased and lacquered into a shoulder-wide pageboy, strode toward Lilli. This could be none other than the infamous Bunny Wallingham, the wedding coordinator. The sequined shoulders of her purple dress were bolstered by loaf-sized shoulder pads. With each stride Bunny took, they whipped from side to side, clearing a path through the dressing room. The massive and ornate furniture, upholstered in gold brocade, seemed to shrink and pale in her wake. Zack had been right about the hat. Purple feathers bobbed and fluttered from the enormous brim.

Bunny clenched Lilli's hand in a vise-like grip, leaned close, and confided, "Let's get one thing straight. I'm in charge here, not the bride, not the groom, not Arabelle Revington, and certainly not the future mother-in-law, Trudy Faraday. If you have any questions, ask me. If you have any criticisms, chew on them."

Bunny leaned away from Lilli, her back ramrod straight, and smiled through clenched teeth. "My pretty darlings are ready for their pictures." She shooed the flower girl, maid of honor, and bridesmaids toward Margie, who was standing with a bouquet of white roses before an elaborate gold-trimmed mirror.

"Smile!" Lilli said and began snapping pictures. She thought that the maid of honor and three bridesmaids, dressed in shimmering ice-blue gowns, were beautiful. Their glistening hair, glossy pink lipstick, sparkling teeth, and rosy complexions radiated good health. Face it, Lilli thought, that's the bloom of youth on firm skin.

"Smile!" Lilli exclaimed. The maid of honor and bridesmaids sucked in their breath, as if to shrink their already-flat stomachs, and smiled. Each time Bunny Wallingham turned her back, the young women winked at Lilli and crossed their eyes or stuck out their tongues. Flower girl Maisie Dembrowski, the bride's seven-year-old freckle-faced cousin got into the swing of things. She made monster faces, poking up her nose and pulling down the corners of her mouth.

Lilli photographed the horseplay. She also got several rear-end shots of Bunny Wallingham as she bent to adjust the girls' hemlines. She figured the pictures would encourage Margie and her bridesmaids to take up darts. Why not, with a target like that? Lilli enjoyed the chit-chat between Bunny and Arabelle. Bunny, striving for what she must have considered a rich-lady persona, sniffed the air like a bloodhound, and affected a peculiar accent, a mix of Boston, Newport News, and London. Arabelle, who apparently tried to distance herself from Bunny, resorted to folksy down-home expressions that sounded like something Gram would say.

"Let's have a full-group shot in front of the dressing mirror." Bunny barked the words and steered the bride's mother, Rita Schyler, to the right side of the bride and the mother-in-law, Trudy Faraday, to the left.

"Yes, Bunny. Whatever you say, Bunny," Rita said between sniffles and the sobbing refrain, "I can't believe I'm losing my daughter."

At every command from Bunny, Trudy responded, "I have a better idea."

Throughout the power play, Margie constantly checked her notepad to make sure that Lilli had photographed every possible combination of bridesmaids, maid of honor, flower girl, mother, and mother-in-law. Margie established a system of winks and frowns with Lilli to register her pleasure or displeasure with the shots. Bunny then ushered all the women to the garden, ablaze with zinnias and marigolds, for additional photos. After fifteen minutes, Bunny clapped her hands and announced, "My precious darlings, it's time to hide the bride in the back of the church. I'll go muster the men."

When Bunny returned, her shoulder pads leading the way, with the men and ring bearer trailing behind her, she was a completely different person. Smiling, flirty, sweet Bunny had replaced bossy, blustery, acid-tongued Bunny. She tickled Margie's father under the chin, complimenting him on his baby face and youthful physique. Batting her eyelashes, she wiggled past Tim's father, tweaked his cheek, and told him to "loosen up." Cooing and fluttering about like a gigantic purple bird, she fluffed the ushers' handkerchiefs and straightened the best man's cravat. She kissed the ring bearer on the top of his head and sent him into a fit of giggles when she gagged on his mousse. Laughing like a schoolgirl, she brushed Tim's lapels and told him what a sweet girl he was marrying, but that if he changed his mind she was available.

Lilli seized the opportunity. Interspersed among the posed photos, she snapped candid shots of the men. Their expressions were priceless, and Lilli knew that Margie would treasure them. She was heading toward the front of the church when she heard a commotion coming from the parking lot. She saw Zack running between the cars away from the church, toward the lilac and forsythia bushes.

The flower girl's father, George Dembrowski, stopped short in front of Lilli. He was clutching a fancy white handkerchief and had a stunned expression on his face.

"What happened?" Lilli asked.

"I went to fetch Maisie's embroidered handkerchief. Some guy in jeans and a navy windbreaker was skulking around the parking lot. He wasn't an invited guest, not in those clothes, so I asked him what he was doing here. He spat and said, 'None of your crummy business.' He took off. I checked around the lot. The convertible top of that green Miata was slashed to smithereens and the driver's side had been keyed. So I came back and asked who was driving a green Miata. This guy Zack said, 'I am. Is there a problem?' I told him he'd better come see for himself."

"Thanks," Lilli said and hurried toward Zack, who burst back through the lilac bushes into the parking lot. Anger shot from his eyes. Lilli met up with him at his car.

"Did you see who did it?" Lilli asked.

Zack pounded his fist on the hood of his car. "No. But I'm sure it's the same guy who sent you the threatening letter. He's telling me to stay away from you."

Zack rotated his shoulders and tried to relax. "This is a wedding, a happy day. I won't let some sicko ruin everything. I'll straighten this out with the police later."

"I'll take pictures," Lilli offered. "You can show them to your insurance man when you return to New York."

"Thanks."

She snapped a half-dozen photos. When she looked over her shoulder, she caught him staring at her. "What?" she asked.

Zack muttered, "I'm convinced this guy is a real idiot."

"What makes you say that?"

"He thought a few scratches and slashes could scare me away from you."

A car horn honked long and loud.

Startled, Lilli and Zack looked around and saw an elderly man in a black limo jerked upright.

"That man's in trouble." Zack walked over. "Are you all right?" he asked, pulling open the door.

"I'm fine. I dozed off and my head hit the horn," he said and tugged down the brim of his elegant gray cap. "My name's Stanley, Arabelle Revington's chauffeur." He shook hands with Zack and Lilli.

"I'm Detective Zack Faraday. This is Lilli Masters, the photographer. Why don't you tell us what happened."

"I was sitting over there on a bench, reading the newspaper, when some ruffian came into the parking lot. He poked around the cars. I sensed trouble. I came back to the car to call the police. He caught up to me, grabbed me by the throat, and threatened to strangle me. I pretended to pass out. He reached in and grabbed Mrs. Revington's daily-planner book from the front seat."

He gripped the steering wheel. "I decided not to say anything until the wedding was over. I didn't want to upset Mrs. Revington or Margie."

"They should know about this," Lilli said. "Or perhaps we could notify a relative of yours."

"Whatever you do, don't tell my grandson, Franky. He'd come charging out here, tearing around looking for the guy. He'd forget all about his gig. He needs every gig he can get. He's the band's piano player, you know. He's got his heart set on a career in music, and he's talented."

"Okay," Zack said. "But I'll come back later to check on you."

"Thanks," Stanley said and returned to his newspaper.

Zack draped his arm over Lilli's shoulder and walked her back to the church. "This guy must think beating up a defenseless old man and rifling through a widow's car adds to his charm. What a jerk! Anyway, I think we should tell the grandson what happened."

"Good idea," Lilli said as they entered the church.

Trying to put the car incident out of her mind, Lilli shot more pictures. She photographed the priest, the altar, flowers, guests, the processional, the wedding party. Every now and then, she looked out the door to see if the guy in jeans and navy windbreaker was lurking again.

Lilli caught sight of Zack several times, sitting midway up the church, aisle seat, next to that perky blond. She looked even more gorgeous now in the shimmering light from the stained-glass windows than she had in his convertible. Life just wasn't fair. Zack was smiling and thoroughly enjoying himself, while she lugged equipment and snapped photos until her shoulders ached. And, she had to put up with Bunny, who hissed commands at her, like a snake in heat. The more she thought about it, the angrier she got.

Organ music filled the church, signaling that the ceremony was over. The happy bride and groom, lost in each other's eyes, strode down the aisle, followed by the wedding party. Row by row, the guests departed. Lilli saw the blond kiss Zack on the cheek, wave cheerily, and hurry out the door. While the guests strolled over to the reception at the elegant Wyandanch Restaurant, Lilli continued to take photos. She went for every shot she had ever seen in her friends' wedding albums.

Zack lingered at the back of the church as Lilli finished up. "How's it going so far?" he asked as she stormed past, fuming about the blond.

"Weddings aren't my thing," she snapped, juggling cameras and film. She wondered why the blond wasn't there clutching Zack's arm, smiling, blinking as fast and furious as fireflies. "You could help me carry some of this," she said. "Or are you saving your strength to dance with Blondie?"

"Blondie?" Zack asked. Then he slapped his forehead and burst out laughing. "Oh, that blond." He pointed over his shoulder. "You mean my sister."

"Yeah, sure."

"I forgot. This week she's a blond. Last time I saw her she was a brunet. She's full of surprises. You never know what to expect. Come to think of it, she's a lot like you."

Chapter Ten

The Reception

Feeling like a jealous fool for snapping at Zack, Lilli promised herself to be nice, sweet, and cooperative. A new Lilli. Zack would be impressed. He would fall victim to her charms.

Zack was waiting for Lilli on the church steps. "I'll check on Stanley one more time," he said.

"How sweet."

"Last time I looked, he was enjoying the sports section and talking to his cronies on the car phone. He told me to go enjoy myself and quit worrying about him."

"He's such a nice man." Lilli smiled. "I'll find Franky at the reception and fill him in. That's a good idea, don't you agree?"

"Lilli, did something happen? You seem, uh, different."

"Oh?"

"Sweet and easy-going." He shook his head. "You're scaring me."

As soon as Lilli entered the Wyandanch Restaurant, she walked toward the musicians gathered at the bandstand. She spotted the piano player—where else—leaning against the piano.

Tall, skinny, clean-shaven, including his head, Franky was rifling through stacks of sheet music. The neon lights glistened off his shiny chartreuse eye shadow and the silver ring dangling from his eyebrow. He wore a chartreuse tee shirt, with a bowtie painted on it, tucked into a tuxedo jacket two sizes too large for him. Chartreuse sneakers poked out beneath his rolled-up tuxedo pants. Lilli figured he was about nineteen.

The other band members, three guys and a girl, all about Franky's age, were busily setting out their music and testing their drums, guitars, and cymbals. They wore black tuxedos, too, but each had chosen a tee shirt of a different color. The vibrancy of the neon orange, pink, yellow, and blue made Lilli wish she'd worn sunglasses.

"Franky?" Lilli ventured.

Franky looked up, saw Lilli's cameras, and broke into a huge grin. "Shape up, everybody," he said. "Here comes free publicity for Long Island's newest hit group. Oh yeah!"

Lilli introduced herself. Franky bounded to the back wall, rapped his knuckles on the glittery sign behind the bandstand, announcing THE BUOYS, and said, "Lilli, meet the group. Spike, Rocker, Theo, and me, Franky. And, this is our new singing sensation, Angie Angelini. She sings like an angel. And, ooo-haaa, she looks like a babe."

"Cool!" Angie said and fiddled with a pink barrette that anchored her gelled blond bangs.

Franky said, "If everything works out, we're changing our name to Four Buoys and a Gull."

"Cool!" Angie said.

"I discovered Angie in a music store in Riverhead," Franky boasted. "She fits our image. No spiky punk cut, no black-death nails, none of that Euro-trash crap."

"I need to speak to you in private," Lilli said. "It's about your grandfather."

Franky paled. "Has something happened to Grampy?"

"He's fine now, but there's some things you should know." She quickly explained everything, including her suspicions about the man who had roughed up his grandfather.

"You're right," Franky said, when she'd finished. "We'll wait to tell Arabelle. Thanks for your help and the detective's too. Grampy has a cush job. Let's not upset his apple cart. Uh-oh, I'd better go. Here comes Arabelle. She'll wonder what we've been talking about. Anyway it's time for me to make beautiful music with the band. And with that cute little blond gull." He hopped onto the bandstand and slid onto the piano seat.

Arabelle said, "I see you've met Franky. A most intriguing young man."

Lilli nodded.

"And very industrious. He works as a mechanic at Matt's marina during the day and performs with the band at night." Arabelle raised her voice over the sound of the band. "I've watched him grow up. He lives with Stanley in the cottage on my estate."

The music blasted, the dance floor shook, and the glassware rattled.

"I'd better get to work," Lilli hollered the words and pulled a camera from her tote bag.

Lilli enjoyed photographing the reception, which was much more relaxed than the wedding. She recognized only Mary Lou Conklin from the camera shop and Annie Revington among the one hundred and thirty guests.

Margie danced by and confided to Lilli, "Make sure you catch Mary Lou dancing with each of the ushers." She giggled. "They have their orders. I'm trying to help her out. But—"

"It's not working," Lilli finished the sentence. Why would it work? Mary Lou was too busy worrying about her dad's dates. She had no time to meet nice young men. Then Lilli laughed at herself. Who was she to be criticizing Mary Lou for the lack of a social life? When was the last time she had gone out on a date? A real date, not just some party her friends had invited her to? The date with Zack didn't count. It had ended before it really began.

Lilli snapped several photos of Mary Lou dancing with an usher, whose bored expression marred his good looks. Suddenly, Mary Lou stormed off the dance floor and headed straight toward Lilli. "Stay away from me," she hissed and shoved Lilli. "You've done enough damage for one day."

Lilli gasped. "What are you talking about?"

"Don't play Little Miss Innocent with me. You told Hank I gave your business card to somebody who's stalking you. And Hank accused me in front of my father."

Lilli stammered, "That's not exactly what—"

Mary Lou poked her finger in Lilli's face. "I know what you're up to. Gram gave you a free room. And this is how you make it up to her. You want to make me look bad." She stormed off, glaring over her shoulder at Lilli.

Lilli balled her hands into fists. "Some days you can't win," she mumbled and stamped her foot.

Zack and a bridesmaid danced by. He leaned toward Lilli and smiled, "Just when I'd given up hope, the old spitfire Lilli has returned." She growled.

Spike, the band's spokesperson, announced that they

were taking a short break. Mary Lou rushed across the floor and sidled up to Franky.

Arabelle came over to Lilli and confided, "Mary Lou has a groupie mentality and chases after Franky. She's been telling everyone she's Franky's date. She clings to him and his friends. She's using Franky to shock her father and capture his attention. It's not working, but she hasn't figured that out yet. Excuse me, there's Bunny coming this way. I'll head her off at the punch bowl."

Annie, dressed in a tailored aqua silk dress that complimented her tan and her slim figure, stopped to introduce Lilli to her husband, Matt. He was a tall, ruggedly handsome guy with shoulder-length jet-black hair and dazzling blue eyes. Lilli thought that Matt and Zack were the two most gorgeous men at the reception. It was a toss-up. Matt's Indian heritage lent him an exotic air, but Zack had the appealing boy-next-door good looks.

Lilli said, "Matt, if you have time later, I'd like to ask you some questions about the Montauk Indians. I might be able to persuade *Viewpoint* magazine to do an article on them."

Matt's eyes lit up. "That would be great."

"I'm surprised Gram isn't here," Lilli said. "Wasn't she invited?"

Annie scowled. "Both Gram and Bud Conklin were invited. Mary Lou didn't like the idea of Gram dancing with Bud and, as she so bluntly put it, 'making fools of themselves.' Gram and Bud have been taking line-dance and swing-dance lessons. They really cut loose and do some wild moves. Anyway, Gram didn't want to upset Mary Lou."

Lilli frowned. "So she stayed home."

Matt chimed in, "Mary Lou picks on Gram. In my

book, that's a serious crime. Gram deserves the best. And Mary Lou dishes out the worst."

Bunny Wallingham barged into the group and nudged Lilli. "Let's keep that nose to the grindstone, young lady. We're paying you to take pictures, not to socialize with the guests."

Lilli considered punching Bunny in the nose. She wondered if Zack would arrest her for assault and battery. But she soon forgot her annoyance. Everyone was in such a good mood. They sampled the hors d'oeuvres. They enjoyed the scrumptious dinner of shrimp-stuffed flounder. And they danced to the lively music. Arabelle was a godsend, running interference every time Bunny came within five feet.

"Lilli, I think you should take a break," Arabelle said when Bunny went off to speak to someone about the departure time of the limousine. "Matt wants to talk to you. Go on, I'll handle Bunny."

Lilli found Matt and Annie on the back porch, snuggling on a wicker love seat, enjoying the afternoon breeze and their own company. Lilli cleared her throat. "Is this a bad time?"

"No," Matt said, pulling up a chair. "Relax for awhile. You've earned a break and a merit badge for putting up with Bunny. Tell me about that article you want to do. How can I help?"

"I'd like to take some photos to show the Montauk influence in Grayrocks. Gram and some of the locals told me about the Montauk Steps at Clam Hollow. I'll definitely photograph them. Any other suggestions?"

"Yeah, the dug-out caves, near the Steps. The Montauks created steam baths in the embankment that runs parallel to the jetty."

"What are they like?" Lilli asked.

"The Montauks dug out three areas large enough for six men each, then fortified the sides of the caves with stones and made a door of sorts from branches with corn leaves woven through. They dug a firepit in the center. When the flames roared, they added cornhusks and leaves soaked in water to the wood."

"Do you think I could find those steam baths?" Lilli asked.

"You could walk right past and not notice them. Here, let me draw you a map." He took a wedding napkin and drew a rectangle. He sketched in wiggly lines. "The water," he said. He drew a series of raggedy circles. "The jetty."

Lilli leaned forward. "The brick building," she said when Matt drew a small house.

"The Montauk Steps," Annie added, as Matt drew a zigzag line.

"And finally the embankment." Matt drew a line with trees along it. In bold print, he placed three Xs along the base of the embankment. "There are three steam baths," he said, tapping the point of his pen against each of the three Xs. "They're opposite the brick building, right beneath a big oak tree." He sketched a tree that overshadowed all the others.

Annie chuckled at his oversized tree with O-A-K scrawled across it.

Matt handed the napkin to Lilli. "Annie's the artist in our family."

Annie smiled, filled with pride. "And Matt's the historian."

"The doors, of course, are long gone," Matt continued. "The old doorways are overgrown and hard to spot. Gram says you're staying on until Wednesday. Annie and I would be glad to show you the Montauk Steps and the caves, at your convenience."

"We could have a picnic at Clam Hollow," Annie said. "None of the tourists will disturb us. They stay clear of the area." She wiggled her fingers and her toes, which peeked out of her shimmering sandals. "They have delicate toes."

Lilli smiled. "A picnic would be great."

"Bring along a date," Annie said.

"I haven't really met anyone so far."

Matt pulled his address book from his pocket. "Well, we'll have to fix that."

The door opened and the strains of slow, romantic music swept across the porch. Zack strode toward Lilli. He greeted Matt and Annie and then took Lilli's hand.

"Well, how's that for timing," Matt murmured.

"May I have this dance?" Zack asked.

"Yes," Lilli stammered. "I've taken all the pictures, the wedding cake cutting, bouquet tossing. I'm just waiting for them to leave for some limo shots."

"Good," Zack said.

Lilli melted. His hand felt as warm and reassuring as it had last night at the Soundshore Lodge.

Matt teased, "If you two get bored with these sedate dances, Annie will be glad to teach you the Montauk corn dance."

"Oh, you!" Annie gave Matt a love tap. From the grin on Matt's face, Lilli knew the corn dance was somehow their special secret. They were obviously very much in love.

Zack said roguishly, "I'm ready any time any place, as long as I can choose my own partner." He gazed into Lilli's eyes. "We'd better go before the party ends."

Lilli followed Zack to the dance floor. "Have fun," Annie called after her.

"I'll try," Lilli shot back.

Zack slid his arm around Lilli's waist and drew her to his chest. She rested her chin in the hollow between his shoulder and neck. As they danced, moving slowly, Lilli felt as if she had been transported to another world. A safe world. A world where someone didn't run off with her camera, chase her off the road, or send her a threatening note.

As she floated across the dance floor caught up in Zack's embrace, Lilli knew that something special was happening. Looking up, she wondered if Zack felt the same way. But his eyes were closed and he was humming blissfully in her ear. His warm breath tickled her earlobe. She closed her eyes and allowed herself to melt into his arms.

A tug at her shoulder broke the spell-binding mood. She opened her eyes. Purple feathers bobbed back and forth. "They're leaving," Bunny snapped. "The bride and groom are ready to go. Get your camera and follow me."

Lilli pulled away from Zack, grabbed her tote bag, and chased after Bunny. She photographed the happy couple driving away in a white stretch limousine, as the guests blew bubbles and cheered. Suddenly, the wedding and reception were over. An unexpected feeling of loneliness overcame Lilli. It was the way she felt on New Year's Eve when the horns were done blowing and the confetti had settled on the floor. A let-down feeling, a blue mood overcame her, as if some incredibly joyful moment had slipped away and would never return. Tears formed in her eyes, and she felt foolish, crying now that the wedding of two people she hardly knew was over.

"Come on," Zack said. "My car's in terrible shape but

it will get you back to Baywatch Inn. Tim and Margie said you're a treasure. They insist that I treat you like royalty. It's a rough job, but somebody has to do it."

Gram greeted Lilli and Zack in the Baywatch lobby with a big smile. She was wearing a canary-yellow tee shirt tucked into her black spandex bike shorts. She pulled off the yellow sweatband that clung to her forehead beneath her bangs.

"Been out riding?" Zack asked.

"Heck no," Gram replied. "Bud and I were in the back yard practicing our aerials for the swing-dance social next week. Whew-eee! We are getting good!" She chuckled. "He's gone to get his bike. We thought we'd take a spin before the storm blows in. Bud figures we'll have the wind at our backs coming or going. That's Bud for you, the practical optimist. He's never figured it's bound to be against us one of the ways."

"He's a very nice man," Lilli said. Then she turned to Zack. "I'll say goodbye. I'm going to stow these rolls of film in my room. Thanks for the ride."

"Hey," his hand brushed against her arm. "Maybe we could do something. You know, hang out for awhile."

"I'd like that, but I have to make up for lost time. I'm going to throw on my jeans and head to the beach. I want to finish some shots of the jetty area."

"I'll go with you," he said. He looked out the front door at the black clouds forming. "Could be a squall blowing in."

"Great," Lilli said. "I don't want all sunshine pictures. The contrast will be good. The wind bending trees and kicking up sand creates great atmosphere shots."

"Well, I don't want to miss that," Zack said. "I'll change, find a dry spot to park my car, and be right back.

I'll carry your cameras, hold an umbrella over your head, whatever you want."

She laughed. "That's not necessary."

"I insist. You helped out Tim."

"I enjoyed photographing the wedding. Young love is fun to be around."

Zack said, "Love of any kind is fun to be around." His mouth turned up in a shy smile. "Actually it's better to be in the middle of it, not around it."

Gram came out of her office, carrying a navy-blue slicker and rain hat. "Here, Lilli, take these. I won't be needing them. And here's gloves for both of you."

"How did you know I'd be going?" Zack asked.

"I know how persistent you were in *Sabrina*," Gram said. "The gloves are in case you decide to climb over the jetty. Ever since that rock-climbing craze caught on, people have been trying it. At least you'll save the skin on your hands."

Lilli snapped open the rain hat.

"It ties under the chin, like a baby's bonnet," Gram said. "It's not very fashionable, but you'll thank me when you stay dry in the storm that's brewing."

The phone rang. "Now who could that be?" Gram wondered and reached for the receiver. Lilli had started up the stairs when she heard Gram say, "I don't believe it! Who would do such a thing? Forget the bike ride. Wait right there at your shop for Hank. I'm coming over."

"What's wrong?" Lilli asked, returning to the reception desk.

Gram stood there with the receiver dangling from her hand. "Bud's camera shop was broken into. Nothing's stolen as far as he can tell, but the photos in his dark room are all mixed up. Somebody tore through them in a big hurry."

Lilli sputtered, "It's him! He wants my photos. I know it." She punched the air with her fists. "He couldn't get into my room, so now he's tried Bud's shop."

"Calm down," Zack said, folding Lilli into his arms. "We'll look through your photos again. We'll spot what he's looking for."

"At least the negatives are safe," Lilli said.

Gram slammed down the phone. "Let's make sure." She ran to her office, pulled up the rug, grabbed the key from the drawer, and opened the safe. "I don't believe it!" She rocked back on her heels. "The negatives are gone!"

Lilli sputtered, "When I get my hands on him, I'll—"

"Was anything else taken?" Zack asked, anxiously peering into the safe.

Gram poked through the papers. "No. I don't think so."

Lilli fumed. "How could one guy be everywhere at once?"

"He has an accomplice!" Gram exclaimed.

"Or our thief is someone with a different motive altogether," Zack said. "Someone who knew the safe was there and where the key was kept."

"Like who?" Gram asked.

"Like Mary Lou Conklin!" Lilli exclaimed.

"Mary Lou is my guess, too," Zack said. "She's trying to stir up trouble."

"And she's doing a good job of it," Gram said.

"Does Mary Lou know about the safe?" Zack asked.

"She sure does. She helped her father install it. And complained every minute about how long it was taking him. Daddy's little helper. Ha!"

"I'm not going to stand here and cry over spilled milk," Lilli said. "Forget the photos. Forget the negatives. We'll go for the real thing. The beach. The jetty. The brick building. The center of town. That's what I photographed. There's something there he doesn't want us to see."

"I'll be back in ten minutes," Zack said. "We'll get to the bottom of this."

Gram said, "I'll keep a watch on Lilli until you return. Then don't let her out of your sight."

"Not on your life," Zack said and hurried out the door.

Chapter Eleven

The Brick Building

"Here comes the storm you wanted," Zack said as he scanned the churning waves and the dark clouds gathering in the smoky sky.

"I'll have to move fast," Lilli said and began taking shots of tourists, who were scrambling to beat the rain.

Scooping up their gear, parents reined in their children and headed toward the street. Their shirts and cover-ups billowed then slapped against their backs as the whipping wind changed direction. Several darted after their hats, which rolled like tumbleweeds and lodged in the brambly grass near the parking lot.

"This is great," Lilli hollered into the wind. She clicked several photos of a sun-burned boy chasing after his beach ball, catching it, only to surrender it again to a sudden gust.

Zack zipped up his windbreaker as huge raindrops spattered his face and hit Grayrocks Beach.

"Come on," Lilli shouted. "I want to go beyond the jetty and photograph the brick building and some Montauk Indian sites that Matt told me about." She pulled on Gram's hat and rain slicker. "We'll keep our eyes peeled for anything suspicious, anything that I might have photographed yesterday that this guy might not want me to see."

"You've got a good eye for detail. My detective skills should count for something. We'll spot it, whatever it is." Zack grinned. "You look good in that sou'wester. Sort of like the lady on the box of Mrs. Jones's frozen fish dinners."

"That's just swell," Lilli said, looking up at him. Several raindrops rolled from the brim of her hat, ran down her nose, and landed on her chin. "Let's go before the skies open up. And before you think of any more compliments to send my way."

Fighting the gusting wind and flying sand, they reached the jetty and pulled on their gloves. Leading the way, Lilli began climbing up the slippery rocks of the jetty. Near the top, which rose about ten feet from the sand, she lost her footing. "Watch out!" she yelled, slipping, grasping for a toehold, as several rocks tore loose. Zack pulled to the side just in time and watched the rocks roll past him.

"Sorry," Lilli said. "There isn't much tread on these sneakers." She tested the rocks, determined to reach the top. She slipped again and her foot landed squarely in Zack's chest. "Ooops!"

"Being with you brings back memories of my days training in the police academy," Zack quipped. "You know, they tried to prepare us for the dangers that lurk in the real world. I'll have to tell them to update their manuals. Here, I'll give you a boost."

"I can handle this myself," she said, gripping the jagged rocks.

"It's a self-defense move on my part," Zack said. He steadied himself and braced his shoulder against the back of Lilli's thighs. Mustering her strength, Lilli reached up and grabbed onto a large gray stone, firmly planted along the ridge of the jetty. She pulled her knees up in a semi-crouch. Zack gave her a final push. She felt his hands grasp her hips, squeeze, and then release as she catapulted over the top.

"Come on, slowpoke," she said, trying to ignore her embarrassment.

"I'm doing the best I can," Zack said. "I had my hands full." He grappled with the rocks along the ridge, swung himself over, and lowered himself to eye-level with her. They sat side by side on the rocks, catching their breath.

"There's nothing red near the building," Lilli said. "Red flashes ruined three of my photos of the building. Whatever it is, it's gone. I thought it was a bird or candy wrapper or something. Gram said it looked like a ribbon from a kite tail."

"Or maybe from a woman's pony tail." Zack's eyes held hers. "Wasn't Betty Morgan wearing red?"

Lilli nodded. "A red clingy blouse."

Lilli remembered the pictures of Betty Morgan she had seen at Baywatch Inn when she'd hidden in the bathroom. Betty Morgan wore headbands, the way women did in the sixties. "Oh, my," Lilli said. "It could be Betty Morgan's head band. If so, then she's been near the building."

"Let's check it out."

They picked their way down the jetty. Lilli stumbled. Grabbing hold of Zack to break her fall, she said, "It's so much steeper on this side." She realized that Clam Hollow was shaped like a huge rectangular crater, with the jetty forming one of the longer sides.

Opposite the jetty, on the far side of Clam Hollow, rose a steep embankment lined with a barbed-wire fence threaded through the trees. On the third side, one of the shorter sides, between the jetty and embankment, gray-green ominous water roiled. The fourth side was a continuation of the embankment, but much steeper and reinforced with a man-made wall constructed of cement and stones. The wall was higher than the jetty and ascended to Bay Street, parallel to the water.

Lilli marveled at the thirteen slabs of the Montauk Steps, carved into the slope of the embankment, and supported by the wall. The steps rose majestically from the beach to the street above, which was lined with sawhorse barricades and ropes festooned with pink plastic triangles flapping in the breeze. She shifted her gaze toward the embankment, searching for any sign of the caves. Nothing caught her eye.

She and Zack struggled through the sand toward the brick building. They circled around to the heavy metal door, which faced the Montauk Steps.

"Let's see what's inside." Lilli turned the knob. No luck.

Zack tugged at it. "It won't budge."

He leaned forward and pressed his ear against the door. "The door is vibrating! Someone's in there!"

He spread his feet, steadied himself, and gripped the doorknob with both hands. "Stand back!" He turned the knob and yanked hard. The door flew open, nearly knocking him to the ground.

On the cement floor lay Betty and Clarissa Morgan, facing each other, their mouths covered with duct tape, their wrists and ankles bound. A necktie connected each woman's wrists and ankles behind her back. Frightened, whimpering, their eyes as big as saucers, they wriggled, trying to free themselves from the ropes that tied them to the metal rod that ran along the baseboards of their tiny cramped prison. Tears streamed down they faces.

"That sick son of a—" Zack muttered. He crouched near Betty and Clarissa. "You're safe now," he said tenderly. "I'm Detective Zack Faraday and this is Lilli Masters. Give her a minute to photograph you." He turned to Lilli. "Get them from every angle." He said to the women, "We don't want to ruin the evidence. There could be clues in the way he tied you up."

They nodded their okay. Mascara streamed down Betty's face. Clarissa's cheeks filled with air, her nostrils flared. She was very agitated and it looked like she was trying to kick her mother.

"I'll go as fast as I can," Lilli promised. She remembered her own fear when as a girl she'd been accidentally locked in a darkroom and thought she would die. This was horribly cruel. And intentional!

Crouching in the confined space, Lilli photographed Betty, then Clarissa, then both. "Done," she said and set the camera in her tote bag.

The women nodded and blinked their eyes. Appreciation shone through their tears. Zack and Lilli ripped the tape from their mouths.

"Thank God, you found us," Betty sobbed as Lilli and Zack untied the knots. Lilli grabbed her Swiss Army knife and slashed through the rope. Betty wailed, "I've been praying someone would pull us from this God-forsaken hell-hole."

Lilli pulled the bottles of water from her tote and offered them to Betty and Clarissa.

"It's all her fault," Clarissa said, gulping the water and

nodding toward her mother. "The creep said he'd take us for a moonlit ride in his boat. He said he kept it down here near the building. My mother fell in love with the moonlight cruise idea. He flicked on a flashlight and led us down those big steps. Next thing you know, he had me in a stranglehold with a knife at my throat."

"What could I do?" Betty sobbed. "He would have killed her right before my eyes. I did what he said."

"Yeah," Clarissa snarled. "She let him tie us up and drag us inside. She never listens to me. I told her that guy was trouble. But she kept looking at the moon. Geeze, Ma. Get a life!"

"You're safe now," Zack said, pulling away the ropes. Lilli stashed them along with the neckties in her tote bag.

Clarissa curled her lip. "That creep'll be back real soon." Her voice was high-pitched, eerie.

Zack froze. "What are you saying?"

"He came yesterday, three times. He's been here once today."

"Are you sure?" Zack helped the women sit up. Lilli began rubbing their wrists and ankles. "It's dark in here. You could be disoriented."

"I'm sure," Clarissa snapped. "He made a big deal of telling us the day and time when he checked on us. He liked watching us squirm as he ticked off the days. He's a wacko calendar freak with crazy eyes. I saw him check off Friday on his calendar when he tied us up. Saturday, he checked us three times. Sunday, today, once."

Betty added, "He kept talking about Monday, bye-bye day. And he has a camera. He took Polaroid pictures of us."

Clarissa chimed in, " 'Smile,' he said, like we were posing for prom pictures. Yeah, sure! Friday the thirteenth prom night!"

Betty said, "He called himself our keeper. He peeled back the tape, stuck a straw in our mouths and gave us thirty seconds to sip water. He shoved dry bread in our faces. 'Bread and water for my prisoners,' he said, taunting us."

"The rotten lousy creep," Clarissa spat the words. "We had to pee in our pants."

The muscles in Zack's jaw tightened. "Lilli, this guy is caught up in some kind of time-frame ritual. We have to get Betty and Clarissa out of here. Come on, easy does it, try to stand up," he said helping Betty to her feet.

Lilli gripped Clarissa around the waist and tried to pull her up.

The women staggered, their knees buckled. Zack looked at Lilli. "They can't make it over the jetty," he said quietly.

"The Montauk Steps?" Lilli knew that Betty and Clarissa couldn't climb them as soon as the words tumbled out.

"We'll die here," Betty said.

"It's all your fault," Clarissa mumbled.

Zack said, "If he sees us, he'll run. I want him, bad. We need to surprise him. We all need to work together on this."

"The caves!" Lilly exclaimed. She pulled the wedding napkin from her tote bag. "Matt drew me a map of some old Montauk dug-outs. They're real close." She slapped her hand against the napkin. "We can make it that far."

Zack looked over her shoulder at the drawing. "Let's go! Betty, Clarissa, are you up for this?"

"I am," Betty said, "I want to see the look on his face when he sees us free as birds."

Clarissa nodded. "I want to slap him up the side of the head and kick his butt. And then—"

"Save your strength," Zack said. "We have to get you into the dug-out. Lilli, this is a tough call, but the best plan is for me to stay here to defend the women in case the guy returns. You take the Montauk Steps and go for help. Get Hank and the Boys in Blue. Be careful. Real careful. And warn Hank, too." He looked into Lilli's eyes. "The sooner you get out of here, the better. We can't have you running into the guy on those steps."

Struggling, mustering every ounce of strength, Betty and Clarissa headed for the caves, leaning on Zack and Lilli for support. The women stumbled and tripped, but they realized that everything depended on their getting out of sight and into a cave before their abductor returned. No one spoke. They didn't waste energy talking and they didn't want to be heard.

They soon reached the embankment. "I don't see any cave openings," Zack said.

"They're beneath a large oak tree, the largest one around." In the gathering darkness, Lilli scanned the tree line. "There," she said, pointing a short distance toward the water. They took a few steps toward the tree.

"I'm getting soaked," Clarissa complained. "Are you sure you two know what you're doing?"

"This could be it," Zack said. He helped Betty to the embankment. He shoved aside the remains of a battered rowboat. The gaping mouth of the cave opened before them.

Crouching, they made their way into the damp, musty cave. Several feet from the entrance, Betty collapsed. "I can't go any further."

"You don't have to," Zack said. "We're in far enough. No one can see us."

Clarissa sank to her knees and tried to catch her breath.

"I can't wait to tell Daddy what a rotten vacation this turned out to be."

"Your father is worried sick about the two of you," Lilli said. "He's at Baywatch Inn right now waiting for you." Lilli pulled Gram's blueberry muffins from her tote and gave them to the women.

Zack's voice turned husky. "Lilli, it's time for you to go." He crouched near Betty and Clarissa, "And from now on, I don't want either of you to say a word. If I have to leave you, for any reason, don't come out until the police are here. Is that understood?"

"Yes," they murmured in the darkness. "And, Lilli, don't tell anyone what's going on here. It will only bring a crowd, or worse, a panicky crowd. That's a criminal's best escape hatch."

"I understand," Lilli said, impressed by the reassuring and calm way he took control of the situation.

As Lilli stepped past Zack, he pulled her toward him. He wrapped his strong arms around her and kissed her hard on the lips. "Get out of here and don't come back. I don't want anything to happen to you. This is serious."

With the sensation of his warm lips still lingering on hers, Lilli stashed her tote bag next to Betty and shoved her Swiss Army knife in her pocket. She peered out of the cave, and then darted into the rainy darkness, staying close to the embankment. The beating of her heart sounded to her ears like Indian drums.

Chapter Twelve

The Montauk Steps

Taking a deep breath, Lilli took off, running along the base of the embankment, avoiding the open stretch of beach on view to anyone looking down from the top. Thunder rumbled in the distance. It came closer, louder, and more urgent, like a train out of control, unstoppable, on a collision course with anything or anyone that got in its way. Streaks of lightning slashed the dark skies, then retreated.

Taking advantage of the semi-darkness, Lilli darted away from the embankment and made a beeline toward the Montauk Steps. Catching her breath at the bottom step, she looked back. The mouth of the cave was shrouded in darkness. Zack, Clarissa, and Betty were out of sight. They were safe, for the moment.

Lilli began climbing the rain-soaked steps, afraid to blink, breathe, or make a sound. Avoiding the open side, which had a sheer drop to the sand below, she came up the side carved from the embankment. She stayed in the deep shaft of shadows, where an overhang blocked the dim glow from the streetlights above. Climbing the slippery steps, which were deeper and higher than she'd realized, was more grueling than her Stairmaster workout. Afraid she might stumble and fall, she bent down and gripped each step with her hands, sort of half-crawling toward the top. She looked over the edge and saw broken bottles littering the sand the entire length of the steps. She figured that kids threw down stones from the street using the bottles for target practice.

Suddenly, huge bursts of lightning illuminated the steps, catching her in their glare, like floodlights on a stage. Heart pounding, she flattened herself against the embankment and prayed. She listened. Was he coming? Had he seen her? The only sounds she heard were the rain pelting the stones and the oak branches creaking in the howling wind.

Lilli started out again. Three steps from the top, she heard the whine of a car's engine. Then squealing brakes. An engine sputtered and quit. She summoned her courage and went for broke, scrambling up the last three steps.

At the top, she crouched in the dim light from the streetlight. She looked left and right. No people. No traffic. The rain had driven everyone indoors. No police cars patrolled. Where were the Boys in Blue? Where was Hank? She took one last look at the sand far below her and the perilous Montauk Steps that descended to it. She ducked under the ropes, climbed around the sawhorse barricades, and stepped onto the sidewalk. Turning right, she hurried along Bay Street, back toward town.

She remembered that Steve and Patty's Towel Shoppe was nearby, about three or four blocks ahead. She would go there and call the police. It must be almost six o'clock.

The shop might be closed. Please be open, please be open, she thought with every step as she sloshed through puddles.

She gasped. Across the street, a man was getting out of his truck. A gray truck. In the rain, it looked slick, almost shiny, not oxidized. She wasn't sure if it was the truck that had tried to run her off the road. The man crossed the street and was coming toward her. Too late. She couldn't hide. She couldn't run. She saw his New York Yankees baseball cap. He was wearing a black windbreaker, his hands thrust into his pockets. She had no doubts. He was the man who had abducted Betty and Clarissa Morgan and intended to murder them. Keeping her head low, she prayed he wouldn't recognize her.

He passed by, inches from her. From the corner of her eye, Lilli saw his sneakers. Not sneakers. Those popular suede street shoes. In the split second that his shoes passed within her range of vision, she noticed the black upper part, the white laces, the name-brand B.U.M. on the tongue, and the wide white reflective band along the bottom.

Knees shaking, Lilli willed herself to keep going. She must find Hank and the Boys in Blue. Zack was trapped in the cave with two defenseless women. Torn between capturing the guy and keeping them safe, Zack would take risks. The guy could be armed, and when he discovered his prey missing, he would unleash his fury on Zack. Zack was laying his life on the line. Saving him was up to her.

Lilli was now directly opposite the truck. Crossing the street, she glanced back as if to make sure no traffic was coming. The man was approaching the Montauk Steps. She ducked down behind his truck. She grabbed her Swiss Army knife and flicked open the largest blade. She slashed both rear tires. He wasn't going anywhere in that truck! Breathing hard, fighting the urge to scream for help, she hurried to the towel shop.

"Lilli!" Steve greeted her at the door. "I hardly recognized you in that rain gear."

Patty dropped the towel she was folding. "You look like you've seen a ghost."

Lilli gulped for breath. "I need your help. Call Hank. Get the Boys in Blue. Fast. Zack's trapped in Clam Hollow. Betty and Clarissa Morgan are hurt. The guy who kidnapped them is on his way there now. He—"

Steve, who had already picked up his phone and dialed the police station, passed the receiver to Lilli. "Tell Hank. I'll get a flashlight. We'll go back. We'll help Zack until Hank gets there."

The phone rang and rang in Lilli's ear. An answering machine clicked on. Static. Then Hank's voice, "Please leave a message." She slammed down the phone. "I'm calling Gram."

Gram picked up on the first ring. Lilli quickly explained everything that had happened. Then, she listened to Gram. As the horrible realization of Gram's words sunk in, she clasped her hand over her mouth to stop her cries of disbelief.

"Hurry, Gram," Lilli finally blurted into the phone. "We're counting on you." She hung up. "Don't expect any patrol cars," she said to Steve and Patty, and headed toward the door. "There was an oil-spill accident on Soundshore Road. Hank and the Boys in Blue are up there with the ambulance and fire trucks. No one's getting in or out of Grayrocks. We're on our own, until Gram reaches Hank. She's taking her bike, in case she can't get close enough by car."

Steve pulled on his rain slicker and grabbed a flashlight.

"Patty, lock up. Turn out the lights and stay inside. Keep calling the police. If you see a patrol car, flag it down."

Patty's eyes grew large. "Be careful, both of you!"

Lilli and Steve raced out the door. As they crossed the street, Lilli looked over her shoulder. The lights in the shop went out. She felt guilty, putting Steve in the dangerous situation of going off to face a murderer. She realized how torn Steve must be, leaving Patty alone in the dark with a maniac on the loose.

Running as fast as she could, Lilli could barely keep up with Steve's loping strides. Crossing over to the Montauk Steps, Steve slipped and fell in a pile of wet sand in the gutter. Lilli caught up. She saw the sign, *Out of respect to Montauk Indians, please do not disturb this site.* She didn't know whether to laugh or cry.

Lilli and Steve crawled over the barricades and ducked beneath the ropes. Steve pulled his flashlight from his pocket. "Let's not use them unless we have to," Lilli said. "We don't want to give ourselves away."

"Okay. Stay a couple steps behind me," Steve whispered. "If you slip—"

Lilli shuddered. "I'll crash into you and we'll both fall off. It's a long drop and there's lots of broken glass."

Steve stepped onto the first stone slab. The wind howled and Lilli clung to the embankment wall, giving him time to get ahead. Holding her breath, she leaned slightly to her left and peered over the edge of the steps. In the misty darkness, she could barely make out the brick building. There was no sign of Zack or the Morgan women or the guy in the baseball cap. Had he wounded Zack and the Morgans? Killed them? Had he seen Steve and her on the steps? He could be lurking in the shadows at the bottom of the steps, waiting to attack them. She had to put all that out of her mind. She must focus on the steps. Everything depended on getting safely to the bottom.

"Okay," Steve whispered. "Come ahead." Lilli had climbed down the first half-dozen steps when lightning ripped across the water. She looked down. Zack was crawling near the building, on his hands and knees. She couldn't see anyone else. Steve was only three steps from the bottom. In a matter of minutes they'd be able to help Zack.

Suddenly Steve let out a blood-curdling scream. He spun toward Lilli, his face filled with horror. "Go back!" he shouted to Lilli, flicking on his flashlight. "Get to the street!" He scrambled up the steps toward her. "The maniac's right behind me. Go! Hurry!"

For an instant, Lilli considered jumping down into the sand. But if she sprained an ankle or landed in broken glass, how could she help anyone? No, get to the street, go for help. Mustering every ounce of energy, she turned and clambered up several steps. Steve was at her heels. "Go! Go!" he urged her onward.

"Watch out!" Zack's voice called to them from the darkness. "He has a knife!"

"Aaaggggh!" Steve screamed in pain.

Terrified, Lilli looked over her shoulder. She saw the guy in the baseball cap pummeling Steve with his fists. Teetering on the slippery step, she grabbed for the wall. Steve hoisted himself up, lunged forward, trying to free himself from the guy's grasp. Lilli didn't have time to move out of Steve's way. Steve crashed into her, knocking her to her knees. The beam from his flashlight spun wildly. Moaning, he collapsed against the wall.

The guy pushed past Steve and flicked open his knife. "You're the one I want!" he shouted at Lilli. He reached for her, but lost his balance and slid on the slippery stone.

The knife fell from his hands, clattering onto the step below him. He reached down and scooped it up.

In that moment, Lilli pulled herself up and scrambled toward the top step. The guy was right behind her, hollering "You're mine! You can't get away!" He flung himself at Lilli and caught her by the knees. She kicked, her foot slamming his jaw. She broke free. He grabbed her by the waist and rolled her onto her back. "You ruined everything!" he screamed. His wild eyes bored into her. He grabbed hold of her shoulders. She kicked and punched, but his grip was ferocious, like steel jaws. He stood up and lifted her clear off her feet.

"Don't! Please don't!" Her words caught in her throat as he hurled her into the night.

Arms and legs flailing, Lilli screamed, "Help!"

Seconds later, Steve hurtled toward her, arms and legs spread like a parachutist in a free fall. They hit the sand moments apart and rolled into a heap.

Flat on her back, Lilli opened her eyes wide and looked up. Lightning flashed. In that split second, she saw the man in the baseball cap at the top of the Montauk Steps by the barricades. He raised his fists over his head and shook them at the sky. He howled like a wounded animal. Then he turned and was gone.

In the distance, Lilli heard the shrill wail of a police siren. Her pulse pounded in her ears. Steve moaned softly. Zack crawled toward them. She saw blood trickling from a gash in his thigh. Steve mumbled, "I'm okay. I'm okay. Get the guy."

"Lilli . . . Lilli." Zack tapped her cheeks gently. "Stay awake, Lilli." He gasped for breath. "You saved my life. That guy would have finished me off."

The beam of a searchlight cut a wide swath across the beach. "Hey, you down there!" Hank's voice rumbled down the embankment from his bullhorn. "Help is on the way. Stay calm."

"Set up a roadblock!" Zack hollered, wincing with pain.

"He's not leaving Grayrocks," Hank hollered. "Traffic's snarled. A three-way collision. Truck, motorcycle, and car.

"He could sneak past on foot."

"No way. I called ahead to the police from Oysterville to Mattituck. We'll get him. Not too many folks out on a nasty night like this. He'll be easy to spot."

Hank blasted into his cell phone. "Officer down. Two citizens down. I don't see the Morgan women. Gram said they were here. Hold it. Two women, near the caves. They're fussing and fuming and carrying on something awful."

Lilli heard Hank's voice far away. "We're waiting on the emergency crew. Speed them up. Let's get these people out of this storm."

Lilli's knuckles and the backs of her hands skimmed the sand. There's no glass, Lilli thought, her fingertips probing the soggy clumps of sand. He threw us far from the edge, beyond the broken bottles. She wanted to laugh, but tears stung her eyes. The last thing Lilli heard before blacking out was Clarissa Morgan saying, "It's your fault, Mom. I told you so, but you just wouldn't listen."

Chapter Thirteen

The Baywatch Inn Lounge

Lilli played tug of war with the blanket, trying to find a comfortable position on Gram's sofa. She was sore, but she hadn't suffered any broken bones, thanks to the sand that cushioned her fall. After a long hot shower, she had changed into her navy sweatshirt and pants, and come down to the lounge. Savoring a steaming cup of hot chocolate, she tried to follow the discussion between Hank and Zack, who were hunkered down in the overstuffed chairs that flanked the fireplace. But Gram hovered over her, chattering away as if to fend off her fear and anger about what had happened and what could have happened at Clam Hollow.

The cuckoo clock chirped nine times, followed by three little peeps.

"Just lie back and relax," Gram said plumping the pillows behind Lilli's head. "It's quarter to ten. You need rest after what you've been through. But don't fall asleep.

132

I'm worried about a concussion. Zack says you're hard-headed, but you had quite a fall."

As Lilli relaxed into the stack of pillows, scenes flashed in and out of her mind. Doctors and nurses. Patty running down the corridor. Steve, a blanket tossed across his shoulders, limping toward Patty. The emergency room. The worried look in Zack's eyes. Zack riding with her in Hank's car from the hospital to Baywatch Inn.

"No one took a turn for the worse, did they, Gram?"

Gram patted Lilli's arm. "Rest easy, Lilli. The doctor said Clarissa Morgan and her mother, Betty, were dehydrated, bruised, and scared out of their wits, but they'll be fine. That guy nearly frightened them to death. And Hank almost finished off the job. He told Betty, 'I'll call my Lizzie and tell her to set two more places at the kitchen table.' 'Lizzie who?' Betty asked, as if she's working up a knock-knock joke. 'Lizzie Borden,' Hank said, chomping on his toothpick. Well, Betty, poor thing, after what she'd been through, threw a hissy fit. She screamed bloody murder about axes, but she finally settled down."

"And what about Steve's ankle?"

Gram smoothed Lilli's hair away from her forehead. "He twisted it, but it's not serious. He and Patty are staying with his family. Steve has four younger brothers living at home, big bruisers, all over six feet. They're safe as toads in a mud pond."

Gram winked. "As you can see, Zack's fine. He lost some blood, but I fixed that problem with a big, juicy steak, a mess of hash browns, and a five-egg omelet. He's good as new, and asking about dessert."

Gram plowed on, "Zack insisted on moving in here to keep an eye on you. I think it's best to call him 'Zack' and not 'Harrison Ford' until everything is settled.

There's enough confusion around here already without bringing in hordes of fans." She chuckled, enjoying her ongoing joke about Harrison Ford. "Oh, I almost forgot, while you showered and primped, the oil slick was cleared. Soundshore Road is open and police officers from miles around are buzzing about town like bees. Hank says he needs a traffic cop to control them and a doctor to attend to the wounds inflicted from tripping over each other."

Gram pointed toward the porch. "As we speak, two cops from Mattituck are guarding my doors and a dynamic duo from Peconic is guarding Lizzie's Safe House. Well, your eyes are glazing over from all my talk, so I'll take these cups to the kitchen and let you tune in to Zack and Hank."

Lilli sipped her chocolate, letting the steam warm her face, and gazed at Zack.

"His strength caught me off guard," Zack was saying. Dressed in khaki shorts and cream tee shirt, Zack looked haggard, but decidedly handsome. When he propped his foot on the hassock, Lilli noticed the bandages wrapped around his thigh just below his shorts.

"I had the element of surprise in my favor," Zack said. "He came to the building. I snuck up behind him. When he opened the door and saw that the women were gone, he went ballistic."

"No surprise there," Hank said. "You threw his train off the track. Plain as the nose on your face, the guy's a pattern freak. He's gonna stick to his patterns come hell or high water, or a nosy off-duty detective."

Lilli detected the concern that sliced through Hank's banter. The guy had knocked Zack off his feet. Zack was younger, stronger, and faster than Hank and Hank's Boys in Blue. If the guy came after any of them, what chance would they have?

Zack raked his brush cut with his fingertips. "He just didn't look that strong."

"Don't take it personally," Hank said. "The teacher who gave us a refresher course just last month has a theory. Her name's Ms. Maloy and she teaches psychology at the community college in Riverhead. She says that men driven by patterns, that's what she calls their routines, are capable of unbelievable strength. They're like lions when their cubs face danger." Hank ran his thumbs along the creases of his pants. "Ms. Maloy would say this guy thinks Clarissa and Betty Morgan are his cubs. He's Alfie, alfalfa, something like that, and you're the rival lion, invading his territory. She says it's the age-old story of a hunter jealously guarding his prey. She made a big deal out of the jealousy bit. I don't buy all her jungle theories, but for what they're worth, I thought I'd pass them on to you."

"Ms. Maloy could be on to something," Zack said. "The guy howled like a wild beast. Then he pulled a knife from his belt and hollered into the wind, 'I'll find you. You won't get away.' I grabbed him by the neck and twisted his arm behind him until he dropped the knife, but he had another one strapped to his ankle. He got me real good." Zack patted his bandages. "I never saw it coming. How could I have been so stupid?"

"Stop badmouthing yourself," Hank said. "You can be proud of what you did. Those women would have died if you didn't think and act as fast as you did. You followed good procedure, you sent for backup." He leaned forward and lowered his voice. "Lilli's got a good brain in that pretty head, slicing his tires and all."

Hank sat back and crossed his arms over his chest.

"And you handled Betty and Clarissa just right. Because of your instructions, they didn't panic and run out of the cave. That was no easy job. That spitfire Clarissa was so angry she was capable of murder."

"Yeah, but who, the guy or her mother?"

Hank chuckled. "Ms. Maloy would say, look first at the primary unit. She means the family. So—"

"Did you catch him?" Lilli asked.

Zack strode across the room and plunked down on the couch. "Hey, you're supposed to be resting."

"I can't until I know the details."

"He's still on the loose," Hank said, pulling a chair close. "But the guys at the station house are working on things. They ran the license plate number from the truck. It was registered to a George Brooker from Smithtown, about fifty miles from here. Brooker had reported his truck missing Thursday afternoon after work, around five-thirty. The guy must have stolen it on Thursday and driven out here that night or sometime Friday."

Hank's eyes glinted with determination. "We're checking the hotels, motels, inns, and campgrounds from Smithtown to Grayrocks. The flophouses, doghouses, and outhouses, too. You name it, we're on it."

Zack said, "While the officers from nearby towns are involved in the manhunt, Hank and I have been rehashing everything, seeing if we overlooked any obvious clues. I'm not much help. I feel like I've got cobwebs where my brain should be."

Hank said, "Don't listen to Zack. He's a stickler for details. Nothing escapes his eyes. He'll help me nail this guy. While all the other officers are doing the foot-work . . ." He rapped his head with his knuckles, "we're using our gray matter."

"What sticks out in my mind," Zack said, brushing

aside Hank's compliment, "are the neckties. He tied them around Betty and Clarissa's wrists and ankles. No fancy bows or theatrics like most of these ritual guys, uh, pattern guys, go for. Just neckties, plain and simple. I wish my head weren't so fuzzy. There's something about neckties I've been trying to remember. A red, white, and blue necktie keeps popping into my mind. One of the guys in my precinct once made a sick joke about a necktie. It's sort of coming back to me." He put his head in his hands and rubbed his temples.

"This could be important," Hank said. "Think hard."

Zack was silent for several minutes, then he looked up. "The necktie had something to do with a murder. July, last year, I think. A teenage girl in jogging clothes was abducted and forcibly drowned. Her body was found in a foot of water in a rowboat on Jones Beach. The coroner figured she was murdered on July Fourth. She was weighted down with bricks, but according to the coroner, she was already dead."

"My God!" Lilli exclaimed. "The bricks must be some kind of fetish. Betty and Clarissa were in a brick building."

"I think you're right," Zack said. "If so, he's got multiple fetishes. The hands and feet of the teenage jogger in the rowboat were bound with neckties. Red, white, and blue neckties."

"I hate to ask." Hank eased forward on his seat. "But what was the sick joke?"

Zack shuddered as if to shake the memory from his mind. "The detective who bagged the neckties as evidence held them up and said, 'it was probably a father ticked off that he got another necktie for Father's Day.'"

Zack stopped when he saw the horrified look on Lilli's face. "It's not like you think. The officer didn't mean any disrespect to the girl or her family. You work these cases involving crazy killers. After awhile, you have to find the humor, or you'll go crazy."

"I know," Lilli said fighting the lump in her throat. "I was thinking of Betty and Clarissa and what could have happened to them."

Zack's eyes narrowed, as if someone had flashed a bright light at him. "This may be a peculiar coincidence. No, forget it. It couldn't be related."

"Let's hear it," Hank said.

"I recall another death involving bricks and a necktie. At the time, everyone in the precinct thought it was a drunken woman sleeping it off, who froze to death."

"Give us the low down," Hank said.

"A storm blanketed the streets with two inches of fresh powdery snow on St. Patrick's Day. Traffic was snarled, but the crowds were as big and boisterous as ever. The following afternoon, two winos warming themselves around a bonfire near a construction site discovered a young woman lying behind a pile of bricks. Her frozen hands clutched a necktie looped around her throat. Her blood alcohol content was high. She had track marks on her arms. No one came forward to claim the body. The official report said that in a drunken stupor, Jane Doe slipped on the ice, stumbled over a pile of bricks, and died there. We called her Jane Doe St. Patrick to set her apart from the other Jane Does in the morgue."

Hank said, "Didn't the necktie make anyone suspect murder?"

Zack shook his head. "The necktie was green with shamrocks. It looked like part of her costume. Green hat, green boots, a plastic harp, you get the picture."

"An ugly picture," Hank commented. "Murder, all

right, dressed up in a pretty costume, to hide the truth. Ms. Maloy would have a field day with this case."

Zack sat bolt upright. "Man! I can't believe we missed it!"

"Missed what?" Hank asked.

"Massapequa. There was an attempted murder on a sailboat in Massapequa, last May. The woman escaped. I can't recall her name—Catherine something, an accountant—but I remember reading the report. The guy tried to tie her up with some kind of silky fabric. She was too upset to remember exactly what. My guess?"

"A necktie," Lilli and Hank said at the same time.

"She helped the police artist with a computerized sketch. I'll have it faxed here. We'll hunt this guy down like the animal he is. Let's—"

"Mother's Day," Lilli said. "I'll bet the woman at Massapequa—the accountant, Catherine I believe you called her—was attacked around Mother's Day. Don't you see? It's always a holiday. Jane Doe on St. Patrick's Day in New York City. The teenage jogger on the Fourth of July at Jones Beach. Betty and Clarissa Morgan on Labor Day here in Grayrocks. And possibly Catherine the accountant on Mother's Day at Massapequa."

Hank jumped to his feet, rapping his hand with his fist. "It could be we've got his pattern. He catches people off-guard, on vacation."

"Right," Zack said. "They're relaxed. They're not alert to danger. They accept the kindness of strangers."

Lilli gulped. "It could have been me. I came to Grayrocks and was taken in by the ambience of a charming seaside resort. Everyone was having fun and I wanted to join in. I was lulled into the peacefulness, the playfulness. I would have gone somewhere with a stranger."

"You did," Zack said. "You invited me for a drink."

"Well, you have a very charming smile," Lilli said. "And besides, you were friendly and very helpful."

Hank chomped his toothpick. "You could be describing the guy we're looking for. Ms. Maloy said killers are often boy-next-door types. A buddy you'd go fishing with."

"This guy picks his victims, probably at random, most likely vulnerable-looking women," Zack said. "Then he counts on the crowds and holiday change of pace to allow him to do his dirty work."

"Father's Day," Lilli thought aloud. "Could this have anything to do with Father's Day? The officer was kidding, but neckties and Father's Day, there's no denying they go together."

Hank sputtered, "Hold on! Father's Day. That's good, but Mother's Day is even better. What we might have here is your classic Mommy hater. Don't think I don't know about this Freud stuff, Lilli. Ms. Maloy, that's the psychology teacher I was telling Zack about, she put a few hand-outs in our sensitivity-training manual. Oedipus, Daddy, and son all compete for Mommy. Family dynamite, Ms. Maloy called it. Personally, I think she goes over the edge on the mommy–son doo-hicky-hooey, but I keep an open mind. If it will help in my work, I'm all ears."

Hank flicked his earlobes. "Now, my wife, Lizzie, is another story. She watches the soaps every afternoon. She believes in everything Ms. Maloy's dished out. She says Ms. Maloy isn't teaching us anything new. She's a bit touchy about my quoting Ms. Maloy all the time." Hank shook his head. "I guess I bragged about her too much. One night at the supper table when I was explaining some of Ms. Maloy's ideas, Lizzie jumped up."

Hank put his hands on his hips and sashayed side to

side. "It's Ms. Maloy this! And Ms. Maloy that! Tell that smarty-pants Ms. Maloy to stay up in Riverhead where she belongs!" Hank chomped his toothpick. "Ms. Maloy has her theories. So does Lizzie. She says it all comes down to, 'the apple doesn't fall far from the tree.' I told that to Ms. Maloy, and she said that I was married to a very smart woman. Well, heck, I don't need no specialist to tell me that. But I have to admit, if Ms. Maloy could figure that out, then she knows a thing or two. So, for now, I'm following up on the Mommy angle. We're looking for a Mommy-hating crazy son of a—"

Gram strode into the room, carrying a tray loaded with steaming bowls of soup. "With all this chatter going on, I figured you're all wide awake. So you might as well enjoy the ham-bone pea soup I made today."

"Afraid I'll have to pass on the soup," Hank said. "I'm going to the station. I'll share my late-breaking news with the cops swarming around. There's bound to be a few eggheads in the group. We'll work this information through the computers. Meanwhile, Lilli and Hank, get some rest. And Gram, no more riding that bike of yours in lightning storms. That screech-owl bell of yours shaved a year off my life."

"Before you run off," Gram said, "let's watch the ten o'clock news. There might be something about Grayrocks." As the cuckoo clock began chirping, she set down the tray and turned on the television.

The music blared and vivid primary colors swirled. A perky blond, who looked like a clone of Zack's sister, announced, "The manhunt continues in Grayrocks, Long Island, and all towns situated between Grayrocks and New York City." She turned to her right, leaned toward the camera, and gave a penetrating look of practiced sincerity. "Do not pick up hitch hikers. That's the warning from Hank Borden, Chief of Police in the sleepy hamlet of Grayrocks. The man wanted for questioning, whom Borden referred to as 'a maniac on the loose,' is armed with a hunting knife. He has masterminded a kidnapping. Possibly he intended to murder his victims, whose identities are being withheld, for their protection. Have you seen this man? If so, call our emergency number."

A sketch of the man flashed across the screen above a telephone number.

"That's my Annie's sketch," Gram said proudly.

Zack said, "It's good. Don't get me wrong, but the sooner we get the guy's name and photo and broadcast them, the sooner we'll capture him."

The blond newscaster continued, "And now, for news closer to home. The mugging spree by a hooded assailant continues in the subways. The mayor vows . . ."

Gram turned down the volume.

As Hank hurried across the porch toward the front walk, Gram said, "Lilli. Zack. My computer's logged onto the Internet already. What are you waiting for? Choose your search engine and start clicking that mouse."

Chapter Fourteen
Mission Control

Springing to action, Zack slipped into the chair in front of Gram's computer. "First, I'll hook up with Digger, a buddy at my precinct." His fingers flew across the keys. "Digger will get the complete file and the computerized sketch, and fax them here. Meanwhile, we'll look at George Brooker, the owner of the stolen truck, and see what turns up."

While Zack punched in information, Lilli flipped through the pages of Gram's desk calendar. "Hmmm. Mother's Day was May ninth, and Father's Day was June twentieth. I wonder if that's when all this really began."

Gram peered over Lilli's shoulder. "What are you getting at?"

"What about Easter, April fourth. Zack, were any women murdered on Long Island sometime around Easter Sunday?"

"I'll ask Digger," Zack said. His hands struck the keys

with a vengeance. "I'll give him some key words, like bricks, necktie, boats, beach. Let's see what he finds."

Gram patted Zack on the shoulder. "You spend so much time working on your detective skills. How do you find time to make movies?"

Minutes later, an e-mail from Digger flashed across the screen. "No murders," it said. "But here's something interesting. A woman reported that a carpenter, who had finished building a porch for her the previous week, showed up unexpectedly. He invited her to go out on his friend's boat. She turned him down. He kicked in her screen door. She ran to a neighbor's for help. He took off. That night, someone threw a handful of bricks through her front window."

Zack punched in the message. "His name?"

"Jack Smith," came back the reply.

"Two points for originality," Gram said.

Zack pointed at the screen. "Here comes another e-mail from Digger." He leaned forward and read aloud, "Brooker, the guy whose truck was stolen, is married. He's the father of three. Owns his own home, three bedrooms, in Smithtown. He's a Methodist, an Elk, and a carpenter."

"Zack, this could be a real long shot," Lilli said. "In all the excitement, I forgot to tell you and Hank something. I think the guy we're looking for might be a carpenter, too. The missing fingertip could be an on-the-job accident with a saw. He's muscular and strong, used to heavy work. And now this Jack Smith incident."

Zack reached for the phone. "It's late, but we'll call Brooker."

"The carpenter whose truck was stolen?" Gram asked.

Zack nodded. "He might know if any carpenters in his union are missing a fingertip."

"Index finger, left hand," Lilli added.

"And we'll get the names of the union leaders. They can fax us their membership list and medical records."

"Fingerprints would help," Gram offered.

Zack added, "We're looking for someone who probably didn't show up for work on Friday. And the stolen truck tells me the guy worked Thursday at the same site as Brooker or nearby."

"He's clever," Gram said. "He does his dirty work on his vacation time, so he doesn't need to explain his absences."

Zack smiled. "But this time he made an expensive mistake. He didn't count on eagle-eye Lilli noticing that red headband and following it up. That could cost him his life."

"You were with me every step of the way," Lilli said.

"While you two make nice, I'll call Hank on the other line," Gram said. "Maybe they've already captured the guy. With roadblocks everywhere and the sketch on the TV news, he couldn't go far."

Lilli stretched. "I need to get the kinks out. I'll straighten up the lounge."

As Lilli gathered the pillows and blanket from the sofa, Gram called out, "Zack, keep working the union angle. Hank says the guy's still on the loose. He's like a snake, slipping through yards, working his way up the island."

The phone rang and Lilli heard Gram purr, "Hello there, Bud."

As Lilli smoothed the slipcovers, she noticed the map of Long Island on the wall behind the couch. Peering at the enlargement of Grayrocks, she saw the familiar names of streets near Baywatch Inn. Her gaze traveled along the map to the tourist spots and then the towns on either side of Grayrocks. Oysterville to the west, heading toward

New York City. East Bay, where Arabelle Revington lived, dipping into the Atlantic Ocean. East Bay was filled with secluded, mysterious names. Hidden Cove. Midnight Point.

Gram's voice rang out, "Lilli. Zack."

Scooping up the pillows and blanket, Lilli hurried to the reception desk. "Is something wrong?" She noticed Gram's furrowed brow.

"That was Bud Conklin. He'd been doing some work in his dark room. When he went upstairs to his apartment, he had a strange message on his answering machine. Muffled noises, like someone in distress, but no one spoke. He's concerned about his Mary Lou. She hasn't come home yet from the wedding. He's tried calling her on her cell phone, but she doesn't answer. And he can't track down her date, Franky. He's the grandson of Arabelle Revington's chauffeur, Stanley. Maybe you remember him? Tall, skinny kid. The piano player."

Lilli said, "Yeah. A really nice guy."

Gram fidgeted with the phone cord. "Bud called Stanley at his cottage on Arabelle's estate. No answer. He called Arabelle and her phone's not working. He tracked down Spike, Franky's friend from the band."

"Had Spike seen him?"

"Yes. After the wedding, the band rehearsed in Spike's garage. Mary Lou hung out with them. Then Mary Lou and Franky left. Franky said they were going to see Arabelle. Something about a used car. Then, it's like they disappeared off the face of the earth."

Zack said, "Is it possible that Franky and Mary Lou went somewhere with Arabelle and Stanley?"

Gram crinkled her nose. "The only place open on Sunday night and swanky enough for Arabelle is the Soundshore Lodge. We can try there. But it's not likely. Franky wouldn't feel comfortable hobnobbing with Arabelle. He knows the East Bay social code. Could be Franky and Mary Lou went there alone. You wouldn't realize it to look at Franky, but he's addicted to Big Band dancing."

"Let's find out," Zack said.

Gram dialed. After questioning the receptionist, she turned to Zack. "Franky and Mary Lou had a reservation for eight o'clock, but they never showed up. What—"

The fax machine hummed. Zack grabbed the document it pumped out. "It's the report on Catherine, the account-ant from Massapequa. She's the woman who was as-saulted on the sailboat and managed to escape."

"Read it to us," Gram said eagerly.

Zack scanned the first page. "The woman, Catherine Reynolds, is college-educated, twenty-eight years old, an accountant with a large well-respected firm."

He flipped to the second page. "Here's her account of what happened from the time of the incident on the sail-boat until she reported it." He quoted Catherine, "Once we were out on the open waters, this guy—he said his name was Harold Jones. He was well-dressed, a professor type with horn-rimmed glasses. He said we needed to trust each other, that was the sailor's code. I know it all sounds so stupid now, but I was on vacation, trying to de-stress."

Zack looked up. "Trust. That's how he wins over his victims." He shook his head and continued Catherine's statement, "I saw rolls and rolls of duct tape stowed in the cabin. 'Are you expecting to repair the boat with duct tape?' I asked and he flew into a rage. He yanked my arms behind me and said, 'Let's get down to business, the business of drowning.' I felt silky fabric snaking around my wrists. I jammed my elbows backwards and caught him square in the gut. He fell back. I dove over-board and started swimming for shore. His rage helped me escape. He must have gunned the engine because I heard it sputter and die. I glanced back and saw the sails fall. He had wayward sails and a dead motor to contend with."

Zack flipped to the next page and continued reading, "I made it back to the marina. I still remember running along the dock, the water squishing out of my sneakers. I was vaguely aware of people asking if I needed help, but I kept going, sobbing, and babbling to myself, a real basket case. For weeks, I was too embarrassed to go to the police. When I read an article about rape in a woman's magazine, the truth hit home. It said if you're the one who got away and you don't do anything about it, you're helping the rapist terrorize his next victim. From then on, every time I saw my mother, or sister, or a close friend, I worried that she could be his next victim. I knew I couldn't remain silent and let him continue his savage attacks. I gathered the courage to come here to the police station."

Zack squinted. "Wait a minute. This doesn't make sense." He pulled the paper up close and read, "At this point, an officer scribbled across the bottom that Catherine Reynolds said she would not press charges even if the assailant were caught."

"Do you believe that?" Zack shouted. He flipped to the final page. "This is an addendum, placed in the folder by a Ms. Annette Kenney, a friend of Catherine's and a social worker, specializing in trauma."

Zack looked up. "I read the original report because the owner of the boat lived in my precinct. But this was included after I read it. Ms. Kenney's addendum says, 'Catherine Reynolds went to the police and told her story. The officer she met with said he didn't want to discourage her, but he didn't think her case would stand up in court.

He said she might regret telling personal things about herself to the whole world, if she lost the case. It wasn't really an abduction, the officer told her, because she went willingly. The guy didn't really do anything illegal. He said he was going to drown her. He threatened her bodily harm. But, according to the officer, that was her word against his. Rough play, the officer called the man's behavior. He told Catherine that a smart lawyer would say she liked it that way and got what she was asking for. Catherine decided not to press charges. She called herself a coward. She found it difficult to be with her old friends and to establish new friendships. She decided to make a fresh start. She moved to another town and is trying to put the incident behind her. I would like this addendum placed in the file to show that the system failed Catherine Reynolds.' "

Lilli said, "Catherine Reynolds was lucky. She got away." She swallowed hard. "This drowning thing is really sick. Is that what he planned to do with Betty and Clarissa Morgan?"

Zack nodded. "Apparently it's part of a ritual."

"Betty Morgan said she wanted to speak to me," Lilli said. "Do you think it's too late to call?"

Gram picked up the receiver. "Now's the time. I'll dial Lizzie Borden's special number."

Seconds later, Betty came on the line. "Lilli, I want to thank you for everything you did. My husband, Ralph, God bless him, he's right here by my side. He said, 'Honey, I thought you ran off like you did before.' 'Don't be silly,' I told him. 'Clarissa and I went for a walk.' " She sighed. "Clarissa's a horror-movie fan. She calls it 'The Walk To Hell And Back.' "

"I'm sorry," Lilli said. "Maybe this is too painful for you."

"No," Betty said forcefully. "Ralph told me not to re-hash everything. But it helps me to talk about it. Clarissa decided that if she survived our ordeal, she'd go on a chocolate frenzy and eat a dozen candy bars. She did, and got sick and went to bed. She's sound asleep, so I have no one to talk to who understands what we went through."

"You can tell me," Lilli said. "Something you say could help us find this pervert."

Betty took a deep breath. "He tricked us into going for a boat ride. He acted like Prince Charming until he'd trapped us. Then he turned ugly, like a mad dog. He liked describing my daughter's death to me and seeing me squirm." Betty sniffled. "He said, 'She'll drown first, before you. The water will fill up her mouth and then her nose. Her eyes will bulge with fear. Bubbles will fly around her head like balloons at a birthday party'." Betty blew her nose. "He wanted me to die twice. We were tied up and trussed like turkeys and that merciless creep was rubbing salt in our wounds."

"Go on," Lilli encouraged. She scribbled 'balloons, birthday party' on a scrap of paper and slid it in front of Zack.

"Clarissa blames me," Betty said. "But it was a beautiful evening, just the hint of a breeze, only a sliver of a moon. The water, so still and silvery, looked like the pond I skated on as a kid. And then minutes later, Clarissa and I were tied up and lying on a cold cement floor. We kicked at the door, just like when you and Zack found us. Once when the guy opened the door, it must have been the first day, I saw my red headband caught on a broken bottle. Please, I prayed, don't let him see it. Let somebody else see it. But at the time, I didn't know if anybody was looking for us. I didn't know if anybody even knew we were missing. We didn't know anybody in Grayrocks."

"Your prayers were answered," Lilli said. "Your red headband showed up in some of my photographs."

"Is that what brought you to the building?"

"Zack was the one who thought it best to check it out. You were very brave to endure two days in that awful prison. I don't know how you kept your sanity. Years ago, I was locked in a darkroom for only two hours, and I went berserk."

"Trying to save my daughter kept me going. I owe my daughter's life to you, Lilli. Clarissa and I mumbled back and forth in the dark, sort of like 'one, two, three, kick.' Don't get me wrong, but I couldn't wait for the guy to come back. It was terrible in the dark. As creepy as he was, at least we had some light when he was there. I could see Clarissa. I could see she was still alive, but I could also see the terror in her eyes. Then . . ."

Betty sobbed uncontrollably. "Then he would leave, slamming the door behind him and we'd be in that awful darkness again. And all I could remember was her wild look. I was afraid she'd snap. I didn't dare cry. I was afraid I'd choke. I tried to free my arms, but they were so badly cramped. How did such a cruel monster ever come to be?"

Try as she might, Lilli couldn't come up with an answer to that bottomless question.

"I'm tired," Betty said. "I'm going to rest for awhile. So I'll say goodnight."

"Another fax from Digger." Zack waved a sheet of paper, as Lilli wished Betty a peaceful night. "It's the computerized sketch of Harold Jones, the guy on the sailboat in Massapequa, who attacked Catherine Reynolds."

"It's him," Gram said. "His hair is shorter and he's wearing glasses, but it's him all right."

The front door burst open and Hank stormed in. "It's bad enough I got half of Long Island's finest playing Keystone Kops in my station house. But the newspaper reporters, TV people, and camera crews, that's just too much." Hank screwed up his face. "Someone tried to slap some makeup on me for a news program. Are they nuts? If I go home with powder on my face, Lizzie will come after me with that axe she's always threatening to dig up from our cellar. She's got an awful temper."

"Calm down," Gram said.

"I can't," Hank admitted. "My station's like a goshdarn paper mill with all the updates and progress reports flying around. They say new angles generate tips, and tips tighten the noose around a killer's neck. One reporter took my favorite coffee mug, the one picturing a fish dangling a person off a fishing pole. Said he wanted to put it on the late news. They're trying to make a joke out of us Grayrocks folks. Well, it's not gonna happen. Me and the Boys in Blue are running what you might call a secret operation. Anything we find out, we share with each other first, then we pass it around the station." He chuckled. "Of course, we leave out a few details here and there."

"I do the same with my recipes," Gram said. "Then I sit back and smile when someone says, 'my blueberry pie didn't come out as tasty as yours.' Course not. Where's the pinch of salt? Where's the squirt of lemon? Don't give away the store, that's my motto."

Hank stomped across the floor. "Worst of all, I have to deal with this grandstander Captain Raymond Spencer. He's the coordinator of operations, sent here from Riverhead, like we wouldn't know how to run things. He's a media hound with PR people guaranteeing he makes headlines and gets on the news. He installed locks on my interrogation room. And he didn't have the courtesy to give me a key. What's this world coming to?"

"I've heard enough," Zack said. "Hank, count me in on your team. I'm off-duty and this is out of my jurisdiction, and I don't want to step on anybody's toes, but—"

"You're in," Hank exclaimed. "Tarnation! I nearly forgot why I came here. A woman who saw the sketch on the ten o'clock news called in."

"What did she say?" Zack asked.

"I just happen to have a transcript of her conversation with me. But the gist of it is a certain Mrs. Janet Franconi, from Port Jefferson, Long Island, thinks she can identify the man. She doesn't know his name, but she says he's a carpenter."

Hank pulled a sheet of paper from his back pocket. "She was patched through to Captain Spencer . . ." He scowled . . . "the handsome, debonair, tan-in-a-can coordinator of operations. She told him, and I quote, 'My neighbor, Maybelle Swanson, hired him to build her porch. Maybelle isn't home now or I'd get his name for you. She drove to Tenafly, New Jersey, to visit her daughter. Maybelle and her daughter, big Maybelle and little Maybelle, go to Atlantic City twice a year and beat the living daylights out of the slot machines. They're in Atlantic City right now, as we speak, taking on the one-armed bandits.' "

Hank rocked back on his heels. "Captain Spencer puffed up his chest. 'See that?' he snapped at my Boys in Blue. 'Publicize! That's the way to solve a case.' "

Zack asked, "Did Captain Spencer get a last name on Maybelle?"

Hank nodded and checked the paper. "Big Maybelle Swanson. Little Maybelle Prescott. They shouldn't be hard to spot. They wear matching yellow smocks with big green polka-dots, with pockets all along the bottom to store their quarters. Captain Spencer has the Atlantic City police tracking them down. Once we have the carpenter's name, we're in business."

Hank's beeper went off. Hank listened for a few seconds. "Thanks," he said and turned to Zack. "Those Atlantic City boys move fast. The carpenter's name is Gabriel Clummer. I'll go back to the station and see what they find out about him."

"Stay right here," Zack said, pulling up a chair for Hank and setting the phone between them. "My friend, Digger, will have more info than you can find on the biography channel."

Chapter Fifteen

The Missing Pieces

"So, Digger, what have you got?" Zack asked.

Digger's growling voice rumbled through the speaker phone. "Your man is thirty-four years old. His real name is Gabriel Clummer, but he has a bunch of fake IDs, including Harold Jones. Long prison record, starting with juvenile arrests for breaking and entering, robbery, assault with a knife. Deserter from the Navy. Married four times, no kids. Violent with women. In his early twenties, he drove a black van with a mural painted on the side, a skeleton in black leather at the helm of a ship, racing her through rough seas."

"What about Clummer's family background?"

"Middle child of three. Hold on, listen to this. His father committed suicide when Gabriel was eleven. Drowned himself in the family pool."

Zack scratched his head. "Anything there about a necktie?"

A pause. "Paydirt! The father was a salesman. Came home one day. Went into the bedroom. Stripped. Left his wristwatch and clothes in a neat pile on the bed. Took several neckties from his salesman's sample case. Walked out to the patio and picked up a handful of bricks from a barbecue pit he was building. He used the neckties to tie a bundle of bricks together and hung them around his neck. He walked into the pool and sat down in the deep end. That's where Gabriel found him. More paydirt, get this. Later, it came to light that Gabriel dove in to save his father, but couldn't untangle the weighted neckties and almost drowned himself."

Digger whistled long and low. "You're not gonna believe this clip from the insurance investigator's report."

Zack said, "Let me guess. Dear old Mom is somehow involved?"

"Yep. She insisted they hide the fact that it was a suicide. She forced Gabriel to bury all the evidence, the sodden neckties and wet bricks, before they called the paramedics. Gabriel, overcome by guilt and grief, waited until just the right moment—like during the burial—and then he pointed his finger at his mother, and started screaming how it was all her fault, that she had driven him to it with her constant nagging about a bigger house, a bigger car, a ritzier neighborhood. Gabriel pulled out the suicide note and, while everyone was too stunned to move, he read it out loud. The mother fainted, collapsing near the open grave."

"Sounds like a script for a horror movie," Zack said.

"And young Gabriel has the starring role. When the insurance investigators swooped down, because the father's accidental death would have paid double but suicide nothing, Gabriel was scared he'd be imprisoned and ran away. When he was found, the juvenile board felt his aunt was a more suitable guardian than Mom, who was still under investigation for the attempted insurance fraud, even though she had never collected the money. Gabriel's criminal career began shortly after. He ended up in juvenile, probation, a string of foster homes, and eventually on the street. That about wraps it up."

"One more thing," Zack said, running his finger beneath the words 'balloons, birthday party' on Lilli's note. "What's Gabriel Clummer's date of birth?"

"It's right here," Digger said. "July 26."

"I can't think of any special significance to that date," Zack said. Disappointment hung heavy on his words.

Digger cackled, "You're gonna love this. Care to guess the date of Dad's funeral?"

"July 26!" Zack rocked back in his chair. "So that's what crisscrossed Clummer's wires? His father wouldn't be around to celebrate his birthday or any holidays?"

Digger said, "And it was all Mom's fault. Gabriel must have thought she conspired with the funeral director to have Dad buried on his birthday. The seeds of paranoia sprouted."

"I get it." Zack sneered. "Let's seek revenge. Let's kill women on holidays."

"Come on, Zack. We've seen serial killers with less logical motives than that."

"Thanks, old buddy." As Zack set the phone down, it rang.

Gram picked up. "Margie? What are you doing talking to me? You're supposed to be on your honeymoon. Have you and Tim had your first fight?"

Gram pushed the speaker button and Margie's rapid-fire flow of words echoed around the room. "Tim and I drove to the Royalty Suites in Smithtown, exactly as planned. We had dinner at the Heritage Inn, exactly as planned. We went dancing at the Rainbow Ballroom, exactly—"

"Margie," Gram said, "cut to the chase."

"Okay. Arabelle asked me to call her when we arrived. She said she had a special surprise for us, but we had to call for the details. She made me promise to call at seven o'clock sharp. Arabelle's answering machine came on for my seven o'clock call, but at eight, nine, and ten, the phone was dead. It can't be the main line because Stanley's answering machine is working, but he won't or doesn't pick up. That's not so unusual. Sometimes he takes out his hearing aids and turns down the volume on his telephone. But Arabelle, that's another matter. I wanted to call my mother, but Tim said once she had the telephone number of our hotel, she'd be calling all night long. I've been trying to get through to you, but your phone's been busy and—"

Zack interrupted. "Margie, this is Detective Zack Faraday. This is very important. Did Arabelle have plans for after the wedding?"

Margie flustered. "Yes. She was going to do a favor for me. Kind of a sneaky thing. I hope she didn't get in trouble with Bunny, or my mother. I hope she's not mad at me and just avoiding my calls."

"Tell us about the favor," Zack said.

"Arabelle agreed to stay behind after Bunny left. Then she and Stanley, her chauffeur, were going to take all the flowers from the church and reception hall to the hospital for the children's ward. Bunny and my mother wanted the flowers to go to their bingo hall. Arabelle didn't really lie for me. She sort of told Bunny one thing and did another, if you catch my meaning."

"So you think Arabelle took the flowers and delivered them to the hospital?"

"Yes, that was the plan. But she would have left the hospital by five-thirty or six at the latest. I mentioned to the concierge and our own private valet—you can't imagine what a ritzy hotel Arabelle arranged for us to stay at—about my needing to make this important call. And they were surprised, too, that Arabelle hadn't answered or returned my call."

"How do they know Arabelle?"

"That's what I wondered," Margie said. "And that's what I asked them. They admitted that Arabelle had spoken to them weeks ago about her secret surprise. The valet let it slip that Arabelle had a brand new car as a wedding present for us and it was at the hotel, hidden in the parking garage. Arabelle had made arrangements to have my old car driven back to East Bay. She was going to give it to Stanley's grandson, Franky, and he was thrilled because he needs a good car to get to all his music gigs. Gigs, that's what he calls his jobs. So everybody was in on this, and it's a wonderful surprise. Well, okay, it's no longer officially a surprise, but—"

"Take a few deep breaths," Gram said. "You and Tim go to bed. I'll drive out to Arabelle's and see what's what. Give me your number there. I'll call you in the morning and let you know. Meanwhile, forget your problems and enjoy the honeymoon."

"A car!" Margie exclaimed. "Can you believe it? It's beautiful. It's bright red, my favorite color. It's—"

"It's time to hang up, Margie dear," Gram said and gently replaced the receiver in the cradle.

Lilli wondered out loud, "Zack, do you think . . . ?"

"Yeah. The manhunt's all wrong. Clummer didn't go west. He went east. He's at Arabelle's."

"He stole Arbelle's day-planner book from her limo," Lilli exclaimed. "He knows where she lives."

Gram's eyes opened wide. "How do you suppose he got through her gates and security system?"

"I'm calling my niece, Corky Monahan," Hank said. "She's a nurse. She works the night shift."

A minute later, Corky's low, throaty voice said, "Arabelle and her chauffeur delivered the flowers. It was plantamonium in the kids' ward."

"Did they leave right away?" Hank asked.

"No. Arabelle noticed a cut on Stanley's head, and Stanley explained that somebody in the church parking lot had roughed him up. Arabelle insisted that a doctor check Stanley. You know Arabelle. The emergency room wasn't good enough for her. She had her own doctor meet them there."

"And what time did they finally leave?"

"Shortly before seven."

"Thanks." Hank hung up.

Zack said, "I'd bet my life they were on the road, and somehow Gabriel Clummer got to them."

Gram paled. "You don't suppose he got to Franky and Mary Lou, too?"

"Jot down Mary Lou's cell phone number for me," Zack urged.

Hank ran his fingers through his thinning hair. "Captain Spencer will turn this into a three-ring circus, but I have to call him. We have a possible hostage situation in East Bay."

Hank's expression soured as he talked to the officer on duty. "Get word to them to come out to Arabelle Revington's estate in East Bay. Fast! That's where Gabriel Clummer is, not in Southold. Not in Mattituck. Not waiting to pose for pictures with Captain Spencer. Hurry! Get them! We're on our way and we need backup!"

Hank hung up. His face was so red Lilli thought he

might explode. "There were several sightings of someone who looks like the guy in the sketch. Captain Spencer ordered the Boys in Blue, everybody, to hit the road. It's a false alarm, but they don't know that. They're as far west as Mattituck. We can't wait. We're going in without them!"

"Take the two officers guarding my doors," Gram said.

"I'll take one and leave one here to make sure you're safe."

A timid voice came from the front porch, "We can't go anywhere without a direct order from Captain Spencer."

Hank stepped onto the porch and bellowed, "You'll do what I tell you. You're in my town, not Captain Spencer's."

"Captain Spencer's in charge. Our jobs are on the line here."

Hank stormed back inside.

"Who has a key to Arabelle's place?" Zack asked.

"My granddaughter, Annie, and her husband Matt."

"Call them. Have them meet us with the keys."

"There's a bridge a mile before you get to Arabelle's," Gram said. "I'll tell them to meet you there."

"Hurry!"

"Done!"

Chapter Sixteen

Rendezvous

Gripping the wheel, Hank sped along Soundshore Road in Gram's station wagon. Thin black clouds, like skeletal fingers, gripped the tiny sliver of moon as if to hold it captive.

"It's eerie on this deserted stretch," Lilli said, from the back seat. She leaned forward, pressing between Hank and Zack, eager to hear their theories about Gabriel Clummer.

"Why do you suppose Clummer holed up at Arabelle's?" Hank asked. "The oil spill was cleared over an hour ago. Why didn't he make a run for it?"

"I figure Clummer's plans got fouled up," Zack said. "I'm guessing he got to Arabelle's by stolen bike or car. He probably planned to have Stanley drive Arabelle away from East Bay, past the roadblocks, once the road opened. His bargaining chip? Franky in the back seat with a knife at his throat. But there's been no sign of them so something must have gone wrong."

Hank nodded. "Maybe somebody didn't cooperate. Probably Franky. He's unpredictable, you know how musicians are, different drummer and all that jazz. Then there's Mary Lou. Knowing her, she tried to scratch his eyes out."

"It doesn't look good," Zack said.

Lilli watched the fog roll across the headlight beams and enshroud the slick, rain-drenched road. She worried about the fate of Gabriel Clummer's four hostages, if indeed things were as they thought.

"Mother Nature is on our side," Zack said, peering through the windshield at the moon-starved night.

"Land's End Lane coming up on the left," Hank said and veered off Soundshore Road. He followed the winding lane for several minutes.

"There's the bridge," Lilli said.

Headlights flashed from the side of the lane. Hank braked. "That should be Matt and Annie." He pulled onto the shoulder.

"Remember our plan," Zack reminded Lilli when the car slowed to a stop. "From here on you drive. Drop Hank, Matt, and me near the gates."

"I know the rest by heart," Lilli said. "I hide the car in the grove of pine trees. I wait with Annie in her car until Captain Spencer arrives with backup. I keep the doors locked and the windows rolled up."

"If we get lucky and bring down Clummer by ourselves," Zack added, "we'll call you on your cell phone."

"I have a bad feeling about this," Hank said. "Captain Spencer may think we're full of beans. He's got a one-track mind. He may decide to continue his manhunt in Mattituck. We could be left high and dry."

Matt and Annie stepped out of their car. Like Zack and Lilli, they were barely visible in their jeans and dark hooded jackets. "There's been a change of plans," Matt said. "We're both going with you."

"No!" Hank said. "We agreed, no women."

"I agreed without consulting Annie," Matt said sheepishly.

"This involves my grandmother." Annie's voice was sharp with determination. "If there's the least little slip-up, the media will say Gram didn't care about the safety and welfare of her guests. Baywatch Inn is her dream. I won't let Gabriel Clummer turn it into a nightmare. I know every inch of the house and grounds. I'm going with you."

"No way," Hank snapped. "It's too dangerous. Clummer has killed before. He'll kill again."

Annie pressed on, "If you want our key to Arabelle's estate, then you'll have to let us both go."

"Annie can pull her own weight," Matt said. "You remember the trouble on Big Shell Island. She saved my life."

Lilli plunked her hands on her hips. "If Annie goes, so do I."

"No way," Hank repeated.

"Lilli's coming with us," Zack said firmly. "I won't let her stay alone in the car. Clummer could sneak past us and get to her."

"I don't like it," Hank said. "But I know how it is with strong-willed women. So, why waste time arguing. Let's go."

"First, some Montauk camouflage," Matt said, pulling a bag of soot from his pocket. He scooped up a handful of mud, mixed it with the soot, and smeared some on his face and Annie's. Zack followed suit and swiped some across Lilli's nose and cheeks.

Hank slathered on the mud like shaving cream. "I wish the Boys in Blue could see this." He rapped the wood paneling of Gram's station wagon. "Come on," he said and everyone piled in.

Lights extinguished, Hank drove slowly toward the cul-de-sac. He eased into the grove to the right of Arabelle's wrought-iron gates. In the pale moonlight, Lilli caught a glimpse of the sprawling yellow Victorian. Its silhouette loomed grotesquely beneath towering maples. Bay windows, balcony overhangs, and steeply pitched porch roofs cast deeper shadows. Monster faces of black holes, gaping mouths threatening from hidden recesses, chilled Lilli as she prayed they were in time. Did such silence mean Clummer had already killed them? Was there no need for light to guard them? The wrought-iron fence, obscured by rhododendron, stretched in both directions away from the gates and disappeared into the blackness.

"We're not entering by those squeaky gates," Matt said. "Clummer might hear us. There's a small gate along the side, hidden by trees, near Stanley's cottage. It's his private entrance."

Hank whispered, "Remember, we're a team of five, and I'm the captain. Stay sharp. Don't take crazy chances. Okay, Matt, show us the way."

"Single file," Matt said, taking the lead. Annie followed Matt, then came Zack and Lilli, with Hank pulling up the rear.

Once inside and after a quick check of Stanley's cottage, they followed the circular brick drive. Staying low, they skirted the flowerbeds and approached the house near the wrap-around porch off the dining room. Arabelle's high-backed white wicker chairs appeared as ghosts circled around tables hovering over bone-white baskets of seashells. Somewhere beyond Arabelle's house, waves lapping against the shore sighed repeated warnings. Lilli's heart raced. Her pulse pounded in her ears.

"There's a faint light coming from the dining room," Annie whispered. "Probably a candle. Could the power be off?"

"Wait here," Matt said. "I'll sneak onto the porch and see what's up."

"I'm going with you," Hank said.

"That's not necessary."

"It's my job, Matt."

"Hurry back," Lilli said. She didn't like Matt and Hank going off on their own. Safety in numbers, she thought. "The five of us should stick together. That's our best chance of catching Clummer."

A strange hissing noise stopped everyone in their tracks.

"Psssssst! Yo, Matt. Hank. Everybody. It's me, Franky." Franky stumbled and collapsed at Matt's feet.

"Are you okay?" Lilli asked, helping Franky to his knees.

"Yeah. Man, am I glad to see you." He groaned. As he tried to get up, he steadied himself by grabbing hold of her shoulder.

"Are you hurt?" Annie asked.

"Tell us what's going on," Lilli said. "Who's in the house? How badly are you hurt?"

Everyone peppered Franky with questions.

"My grandfather's in there. So are Mary Lou and Arabelle. Some lunatic named Clummer hog-tied them."

"Is Clummer in the house?" Zack asked.

"He was when I left."

"Where?"

"The dining room and kitchen."

"I know the layout. I'm going there now," Matt said. "Franky, tell Detective Faraday what you know." Matt took off, quick as a deer, with Hank at his heels.

"Tell me everything, Franky, but keep it down." Zack cupped his hand around one side of his mouth. "We don't want to let Clummer know we're here."

Lilli said, "I can barely make out Matt and Hank. They're sneaking onto the porch."

"Keep your eyes on them," Zack said, easing Franky back to the ground. "You too, Annie. And let me know if anything happens. Okay, Franky, talk fast. Tell me everything before Matt and Hank report back. When they do, we'll make our move."

"I pulled up to the gates," Franky began hurriedly. "This lunatic jumped out of the bushes. He hopped into the back seat, held his knife to Mary Lou's throat, and said 'Pull onto the grounds.' He shoved us out of the car and prodded us into the foyer where Grampy and Arabelle, who had just arrived, were unloading stuff from the limo. They froze when they saw the knife against Mary Lou's neck. He herded everyone into the kitchen. He told me not to move and took Mary Lou out back. I tried the kitchen phone when I figured he was out of earshot, but by then he'd already cut the main line. He returned before I could search for a weapon and yelled for me to rip out the window cords. He grabbed a stack of dishtowels. We knew he planned to gag us and tie us up. But he never got the chance. It happened so fast, I—"

"Tell me how Clummer operates," Zack urged.

Franky swallowed hard. "He singled out Arabelle and kept his knife at her throat. He commanded Grampy to turn on the kitchen TV. We were too scared to move. We heard him ID'd and saw his picture with the kidnapping story. The scumball went ballistic. He twisted Arabelle's arm behind her back and started marching her back and forth. I was afraid he'd stick her right then and there. Then came the news about the roadblocks. 'I'm stuck in this one-horse town,' he bellowed. I said, 'Easy, fella.' He let go of Arabelle and cuffed me. Grampy lunged at him. He swatted Grampy like a pesky fly. Then Muffin, Arabelle's puppy, howled at the back-porch door. The noise freaked the guy out. He grabbed Arabelle again. 'Nobody move!' he yelled, dragging Arabelle out to the porch."

Franky snorted. "Fast as lightning, Grampy pushed me into the dumbwaiter and slid the door shut. You'd never notice it the way it disappears into the wood paneling. The lunatic stormed back dragging Arabelle. 'Where's the kid?' he shouted. I heard Grampy scream and then a big thud when he hit the floor. 'You've ruined everything,' Clummer hollered. I didn't dare move and give away my hiding place. Mary Lou screamed, 'Franky, don't leave me. Come back, Franky. I love you Franky.' The 'I love you' was pure crap. That's when it hit me!"

"What hit you?" Lilli whispered.

"Mary Lou. She was making noise to cover my get-away. Arabelle got the message. 'Franky,' she hollered, 'we need you.' Those two carried on like teenagers at a rave party. The lunatic kept shouting, 'Shut up or you've both had it.' I rode the dumbwaiter to the second floor, just like when I was a kid, and squeezed out in Arabelle's breakfast room. The screaming stopped. I figured he'd forced Arabelle to bind and gag them and then he tied up Arabelle. I opened the balcony doors and crawled onto the porch roof. Motion sensors set off the floodlights."

Franky caught his breath and Lilli said, "Hank and Matt are still on the porch. I can't tell what they're doing."

Franky continued, "Below me was Arabelle's rose garden. And her fancy iron trellises with dagger tips. I wasn't taking any chances. I scrambled to the far side of the porch roof. I sort of scooted my way down until I could almost reach the apple tree and made a flying leap. I grabbed hold of a branch and swung over to the trunk, just like Tarzan, man. I stayed there, hidden in the leaves. The lunatic ran around the house. He stood right beneath me. I thought he'd hear my breath. BOODA-BOODA-BOOM! BOODA-BOODA-BOOM! BOODA-BOODA-BOOM! It sounded like my buddy Spike's jive drumming. Clummer ran back to the house. I started down the tree, planning to run to the cottage and call for help. I slipped on one of those darn apples and fell. I knew my right ankle was broken as soon as I put my weight on it."

"Let's take off that sneaker," Lilli said, untying the laces. Franky groaned with pain.

"I need to hear the rest," Zack said urgently.

"I was afraid I'd black out," Franky said. "So I rolled under the hedge. Clummer ran by every few minutes, ranting that he was going to kill everyone, starting with me. Then BAM! All the lights went out."

Annie said, "He must have found the circuit box and pulled the main breaker."

"That's what I figured," Franky said. "So I rolled out and dragged myself to the window. I saw him in the kitchen, holding a candle, guzzling orange juice. Mary Lou and Arabelle were tied up at the entrance to the dining room. Grampy was knocked out cold on the kitchen floor, bound and gagged for good measure. I waited until Clummer left the kitchen. Then I tapped at the window. Grampy opened one eye. He saw me and winked. He was playing possum, stalling for time until I brought help. Arabelle and Mary Lou nodded toward Mary Lou's cell phone."

"Where, exactly, is her cell phone?"

"It's laying on the floor between them and Grampy, in front of the pantry door. Their hands weren't free to work it and I sure couldn't go in after it."

"Did the phone ever ring?" Zack asked.

"Yeah, twice. And Clummer went nuts, screaming, kicking the phone."

"Does it still work?"

"I think so. Anyway, next thing I know, all of you were creeping across the lawn in your ghoulie Halloween makeup."

"You've done your best. We'll take over now," Zack said. "Lilli, what's taking Matt and Hank so long?"

"I don't know. They're flat up against the wall."

"You've seen them move?"

"Yeah."

"Annie, tell me about the doors," Zack said. "How many? Where are they located?"

"Double doors at the front. To the left, heading toward the rear, there's a summer porch wrapping around to the kitchen. To the right, four pairs of French doors off the dining room and living room onto the large porch where Matt and Hank are. The new east wing can only be accessed through the solarium inside."

Just then Matt returned. Hank came a few seconds later, huffing and puffing.

"What took so long?" Lilli asked.

"I tripped on the porch step," Hank said. "We thought Clummer might have heard me. We held our breath, and waited, just in case."

"Everyone's alive," Matt said. "Stanley and Arabelle seem dazed. Mary Lou's alert, but running out of steam.

"Clummer's another story. He has himself worked into a frenzy. He's got murder written all over him. We need to move in now. We can't wait for backup."

Zack scooped up Franky. "I'll carry you to that clump of trees. Stay quiet until we bring everyone out. We'll come back for you."

"Grampy's old." Franky's voice cracked. "Please don't let that bully hurt him anymore. I never let on to him, but he's one great dude. This is all my fault. I should have reached the cottage and called for help."

"Don't be so tough on yourself," Zack said. "Gabriel Clummer's to blame. And we're going to make sure he doesn't hurt anyone else again, ever. There's five of us ready to bring him down. Come on, Franky, think of the odds. What chance does Clummer have?"

"Right," Franky said, but Lilli didn't think he sounded convinced. She could tell that Zack was trying hard to give Franky hope. Everyone else, too. Maybe even himself.

"Okay, team, listen up," Hank whispered. "We need to rework our plan. It's going to be like getting the chicken, fox, and oats across the river. We hadn't figured on the women. We can't leave them here alone and it's too risky for all five of us to go in, so—"

"Don't change anything on our account," Lilli said emphatically. "We're here to help." She realized how she and Annie had stymied the original plan of the three men going in together. She and Annie had put Zack in extreme danger. She wouldn't blame him if he wanted nothing to do with her ever again.

Zack said, "Hank, if you'll go along with my plan, we can put the women to good use. Sort of a group effort."

"Let's hear it."

"I'll sneak onto the summer porch and get to the

kitchen door. That's as far as I can go without Clummer seeing me in the candlelight. Then I'll call Mary Lou's cell phone. That should rattle Clummer. While he's kicking and screaming, I'll jump him. If something goes wrong and he gets past me, I'll be counting on all four of you. You're my buffer zone. I want you to form a semicircle across the front of the house."

Zack pointed toward the left of the house. "Hank, you'll follow me and take the lead position near the summer-porch door. Matt, you'll be over on the right, by the French doors and dining room porch. Lilli and Annie, space yourselves between Hank and Matt and watch the front door. If Clummer comes toward any of you, shine your flashlights in his eyes and call out your position. Then run like blazes. And stay within sight of at least one other person at all times. Is everyone clear on that?"

"Yes."

"If I nail Clummer inside the house," Zack said, "wait for my 'all clear.' Then come in and we'll free Arabelle, Stanley, and Mary Lou. Is everyone clear on that too?"

"Yes."

"Zack, be careful," Lilli said. "You know better than any of us, what a monster you're up against."

Lilli watched Zack take off toward the house. She prayed he would get out of this alive, without a scratch. She prayed the backup would arrive at any minute. She told herself that Zack, a well-trained detective, had probably engaged in hand-to-hand combat many times with dangerous, hard-core criminals. But Clummer had wounded Zack before. What would stop him from killing him now?

Chapter Seventeen

On Her Own

Zack raced off to the left toward the summer porch that led to the kitchen. Hank followed, eager to take his position at the porch door. Matt took off to the right, heading toward the dining room porch.

"It's our turn," Lilli said to Annie. "We'll space ourselves between Hank and Matt and keep our eyes on the front door. If Clummer breaks out of the house, one of us will spot him."

"Okay," Annie said. "I'll go right, toward Matt."

"I'll go left, toward Hank."

"Good. That will give Zack the semi-circle buffer zone he wants."

As they took off Lilli whispered, "I keep thinking this must be a nightmare I can't wake up from. I'm scared for all of us."

"Me, too," Annie whispered back. "I pray that Arabelle, Stanley, and Mary Lou are okay."

"Pray hard. Clummer's capable of anything and every-thing."

Lilli and Annie scurried across the soaking-wet grass toward their positions in sight of the front door. Annie ducked beneath the branch of a maple tree. Lilli dropped onto her knees behind a clump of birches. The tiny sliver of moon slipped behind swirling ebony clouds.

Lilli looked left, then right. It was so dark, she couldn't see Hank or Matt. She could barely make out Annie who was just a few feet away. The dark clothes and mud-soot mixture, the Montauk camouflage, were very effective. What was going on in the house? Zack must be inside by now. What was taking so long? She hadn't heard a phone ring. She depressed the stem of her watch and the face glowed with a soft blue light. Eleven-fifteen. Maybe Zack had already tackled Clummer and slapped on handcuffs. It was possible. The element of surprise was on his side.

Lilli flicked open the largest blade of her Swiss Army knife. She knew that Annie had brought along her fish-scaling knife. Aren't we something, she thought. Wonder Woman and Super Woman, armed to the teeth with high-tech weapons, ready to overpower a maniac.

Muffled noises came from inside the house.

The candlelight died.

Had Clummer seen Zack? Attacked him? Lilli leaned forward, straining to hear any sound that would let her know Zack was alive.

"Porch door!" Hank's distressed voice cried out. "Clummer's on the porch!"

Thrashing noises through the shrubbery.

Then silence.

Matt appeared out of nowhere, running, pulling Annie with him, and grabbed hold of Lilli's hand. "Get out of here, both of you," he whispered. "Clummer's on the

loose. Go back and hide with Franky. Wait for backup.
I'll lure Clummer toward the trellises. Those dagger tips
will finish him off."

"You go to Franky," Lilli said to Annie. "I'm not leaving until I know Zack's all right."

"Go, Annie," Matt said. "For once in your life, listen
to me. Go."

Annie hesitated. "Okay, hurry. I'll be waiting." She
kissed Matt and took off.

"You should go, too," Matt said to Lilli.

"No," Lilli said firmly.

"There's no time to argue. At least promise me when
we catch up with Hank, you'll stay with him."

"What about you?" Lilli asked.

"Clummer and I have a rendezvous in the rose garden."

Grasping her knife, Lilli followed Matt. They had gone
a few yards when a big ball of fur flew across their path.
Lilli jumped. Stifling her scream, she cupped her hand
over her mouth.

"A raccoon," Matt whispered and her heart beat normally. He held out his arm and Lilli stopped in her tracks.
Crouching, Matt whispered, "Hank? Are you there?"

"Over here," came Hank's hushed words.

Following the sound of Hank's voice, Lilli and Matt
found him, sprawled beneath a towering maple, rubbing his
head. "Clummer blindsided me. I'm okay. Zack is—"

In the same split second, Lilli heard a footfall behind
her and a dull thwacking sound. Matt's anguished cry
ripped through the air. She turned and saw Matt collapse
and heave forward. Twigs snapped. Gabriel Clummer
leaped from the darkness. Paralyzed with fear, Lilli stood
rooted to the ground.

"I should have killed you when I had the chance!"

Clummer screamed at Lilli, wild-eyed, his breath creasing her cheek. She turned to run. He gripped her around the waist, pinning her upper arms to her sides. The fall from the Montauk Steps flashed through her mind. Clutching her knife, Lilli pulled up every reserve of courage. She swung her hand back toward Clummer's gut with all her might.

"Aaaaggghhh!" Clummer bellowed, and Lilli knew the blade had found its mark. He crumpled. She spun free. "Run! Hide!" the voice inside her warned. She staggered, gasping for breath. "Go! Get away!" the voice screamed in her ears.

Slipping and sliding on the wet grass, Lilli tried to run. She tumbled down an incline, rolled over twigs that crackled like thunder, and crashed into a tree. Curling into a tight ball, she remained perfectly still. If she got up and tried to run, the twigs would give her away. She held her breath and peered into the darkness. No sound from Hank or Matt. Had Hank passed out? Was Matt unconscious? Dead?

White streaks flashed by, less than a yard from where she hid. The reflecting tape on Gabriel Clummer's B.U.M. shoes! The streaks turned away and traveled toward the front door. She heard wheezing and gasping coming from that direction. Had she gotten lucky and wounded Clummer seriously? Or was he pretending, so she would give away her hiding place? Where was Zack?

Trembling, Lilli stood up. Clummer's shoes! Coming back. Coming toward her. She couldn't run to Franky and Annie and lead Clummer to them. And she couldn't get past Clummer. There had to be a way. Think, she told herself. Distract Clummer. Send him on a wild goose chase. She scooped up a handful of twigs and flung them as far as she could away from herself and the house.

Clummer took the bait and sprinted after the twigs. Lilli counted to three, allowing Clummer to get further away. Another three and she'd run to the side of the house, to the porch and then the kitchen, the same way Zack had gone.

Mustering every ounce of courage, Lilli raced toward the porch. Clummer shrieked, "I'll get you! You won't get away!" His rage propelled her. Faster! Faster!

Lilli dashed up the porch steps. Across the porch. The door. Inside. Collapsing against the doorframe, she gasped for breath.

An arm came out of nowhere. A hand covered her mouth. Zack whispered, "Hide in the pantry and don't come out until I say so." He pulled her toward a doorway and pushed her inside.

Panic gripped Lilli. She couldn't breathe. She had to get out. She was back in the neighbor's darkroom, where she had been locked in as a child. She was trapped in the brick building, Clarissa and Betty's prison. She would die in this room. She was in her own coffin.

The porch door squeaked. Clummer! Her breath caught in her throat. If she left now, she would endanger Zack. Because of her stupid fears, Zack might die. If only she could see. If only there was a window with a hint of light. If only. If only.

Frantic, she depressed the button on her wristwatch. Light—a tiny glow of light—enough to see her surroundings. Jars. Cans. Preserves. Pots and pans. Normalcy. Order.

Lilli's breathing slowed. She could do this. The light from her watch faded. She remembered Betty and Clarissa's bravery. She didn't need the light. She could stay in a dark confined space and not go crazy. She would be like Betty and Clarissa. She would not panic.

A terrible racket came from the kitchen. Tables and chairs crashed to the floor. Dishes and glasses shattered. Shouts. Zack's voice. Clummer's. There were more crashing noises as Zack and Clummer struggled. And then Clummer shouted, "Up against that door!"

Zack shouted back, "You gonna cuff me to the pantry doorknob?"

"You got that right," Clummer growled. "I'm no cop killer. They hurt you forever for that."

Now or never, Lilli thought. Clummer doesn't know I'm in here. Without making a sound, Lilli grabbed the largest skillet from the shelf and held her breath. She flicked the watch light and watched the doorknob for the first sign of movement. Nothing. Then it jiggled. She burst through, knocking Zack into Clummer. While they scuffled, Lilli hit Clummer over the head with the skillet. Again and again, she landed knock-out blows.

Zack turned on his flashlight. He looked dazed but managed to ask, "What took you so long?"

Lilli countered, "I was waiting for my cue."

Chapter Eighteen

The Bewitching Hour

Everything happened so quickly that Lilli felt as if the world was spinning uncontrollably through time and space.

Sirens wailed, coming closer and closer.

Cupping his hands to his mouth, Zack yelled toward the porch, "Come ahead! Clummer's down!" And then he said to Arabelle, Stanley, and Mary Lou, "Hold on. We'll have you free in two minutes." The beam of his flashlight swirled across the kitchen where Clummer, gagged and handcuffed, writhed on the floor.

"Teamwork!" Hank cheered from the porch, followed by Matt's "Good going, Zack!" Then came Annie's distant shout, "We're on our way!" and Franky's exultant "Wahoo, baby! Party time!"

Hank and Matt struggled from the porch into the kitchen, mopping the blood trickling from their head wounds. Their flashlight beams crisscrossed like swords.

Annie rushed through the kitchen doorway. Trailing behind her came Gram and Bud, with Franky limping and leaning on their shoulders for support. "Where's my Mary Lou?" Bud asked.

Freed from their cords and gags, Arabelle, Stanley, and Mary Lou all jabbered at once, crying, hugging each other, thanking everyone, and cursing Clummer.

Mary Lou sobbed, "I'm sorry, Daddy. I stole Lilli's negatives from Gram's safe and I let that creep, Clummer, have her business card. I never thought anyone would suffer."

"Grampy," Frank said, embracing him and fighting back tears. "Next time you want me to hide in the dumbwaiter, just say so. Then again, maybe I do need a push in the right direction now and then."

Everyone laughed. Stanley pulled a box of candles from the buffet and lit up the dining room like a birthday cake. Lilli breathed a sigh of relief. The tension and smell of fear that had permeated the room dissipated in the flickering light.

Hank swaggered across the floor and said into his cell phone, "Lizzie, the eagle has landed. Papa's coming home. Break out the champagne."

Zack's watch beeped. "Midnight," he said. "Labor Day is officially here. Lilli, it's time we—"

The sirens were now ear-splittingly loud. Headlights flashed in the driveway. Car doors slammed. Voices rang out. A man's deep voice boomed through a bullhorn, "This is Captain Spencer. Stand aside. We're coming in."

The door flew open and slammed against the wall. Crockery clattered. Utensils rattled. Captain Spencer, followed by the Boys in Blue, his PR team, a photographer, and two officers, stomped into the kitchen. "Everybody up against the wall!" he shouted into the bullhorn. "Now!"

"Geeze, put down the bullhorn," Hank said, holding his ears. "We hear you loud and clear."

Captain Spencer huffed up to Hank and wagged his pudgy finger in Hank's face. "I'm in charge of this case," he sputtered, stamping his foot. "And I'll conduct it my way. Now, like I said, everybody up against the wall."

"No disrespect, Captain Spencer," Zack said. "But we're the good guys." He pointed at Clummer, writhing on the floor. "There's the bad guy. And he's one of those unfriendly, uncooperative types. Standing up against the wall probably isn't on his agenda."

The PR man holding a clipboard cleared his throat and ushered the photographer forward. "Captain Spencer, if I may have a moment of your valuable time."

"What is it?" Captain Spencer snapped.

The PR man cupped his hand and whispered something to Captain Spencer.

Captain Spencer nodded. Without a word, he strode to the dining room table. He posed, chest puffed out, gut sucked in, chins held high, flashing his perfectly capped sparkling teeth, as if he were presiding over a press conference. A member of the public relations team, a guy with a blustery red face, shuffled through the pages of his yellow pad and pulled out a sheet on which he had scrawled in big, bold letters: 'Captain Raymond Spencer captures dangerous kidnapper.'

Captain Spencer's eyes glistened. Lilli had seen that look before. Every politician who'd ever stepped on a soapbox assumed that pose. Let him have his glory, Lilli thought. All that matters is that Clummer is caught. Captain Spencer's deep voice bellowed, "Every citizen victimized by Gabriel Clummer can rest easy tonight." Blinding flashbulbs went off. "I invite you and everyone involved . . ." More flashbulbs. "In bringing Gabriel

Clummer to justice . . ." Flash! Flash! "To be my personal
guest . . ." Flash! "At the Soundshore Lodge tonight."

Hank folded his arms across his chest and grinned.
"When you think about it, the entire town of Grayrocks
was victimized. Our Labor Day holiday was spoiled.
You've made a very generous offer, Captain Spencer,
picking up the tab for our grateful citizens. Why, we'll
be talking about you and your generosity for years to
come."

"That's not what—" Captain Spencer flustered. "Let
me restate—" He turned to his PR team.

The PR man with the blustery red face made a big show
of holding the kitchen door open. "Captain Spencer will
clarify his statement at another time. Duty calls. He must
escort Clummer to the waiting hands of his superiors."

Captain Spencer glared. "Superiors? Ha! They are my . . .
Never mind. Let's go!"

Bullhorn dangling from his hand, Captain Spencer
stormed from the room, followed by the two officers who
hustled Clummer along, the PR team, the photographer,
and finally the Boys in Blue, who looked over their shoulders and gave Hank the thumbs-up signal. Hooray for
Grayrocks was written all over their grinning faces.

"Thanks for taking Clummer off our hands," Hank
called after Captain Spencer. "I don't know how we managed until you got here." He flicked his hands briskly as
if he were shedding bilge water. "Thank heavens this
town is back in my hands."

Zack patted Hank on the shoulder. "That's where it's
been all along."

Gram piped up, "Clummer was rotten to the core. According to my latest e-mail scuttlebutt, when he bought a
map of Grayrocks at Slim's Gas Station, Clummer called
us folks 'a bunch of clam diggers and oyster shuckers.' "

"Could be worse," Hank said. "He could have called us 'New Yorkers'."

Zack and Lilli strolled hand in hand toward Gram's station wagon. The leaves of the maple trees rustled in the balmy air. The moonlight glinted off the dewy grass.

"How will this end for Gabriel Clummer?" Lilli asked.

"I don't have a crystal ball," Zack said. "But here's the typical scenario. Motions will be filed. Clummer will appear in court, wearing his glasses, dressed in a business suit, hiding behind the cloak of respectability. Witnesses will be questioned, evidence weighed, lawyers will battle it out, and the jury will deliberate and then decide."

"Your best guess?"

"Well, with the evidence we have and the testimony, I'd say the jury will be out less than an hour. Clummer will spend the rest of his life in jail. Maybe he'll get the electric chair or lethal injection. That will depend on what else is dredged up. Right now, we only know about his rampage through Long Island."

Lilli said, "I shudder just to think of all the places he's lived, and all the holidays he celebrated in his own sick way."

"We've probably seen only a small sample of his rage. I have a feeling we'll find a collection of Polaroids of his victims. A trophy room, that would be Clummer's style."

Zack leaned against the station wagon. "Let's put all that out of our minds and pick up where we left off."

"Where was that?"

"Holding hands for starters," Zack said.

Lilli smiled. "I thought we were way beyond that."

Zack put his arms around Lilli's waist and drew her close. He kissed her long and hard. She matched his passion and threw in a little extra, for good measure.

"It's been a wild two days with you, Lilli Masters. Every moment we're together, sparks fly. I've fallen head over heels, if you know what I mean."

"Me too," Lilli said. "And I fell faster and further than you. It's a long drop from the Montauk Steps."

Zack laughed. "With Clummer out of the picture, we can actually sit around and talk without worrying about being pushed, shoved, punched, or stabbed."

Lilli put her arms around Zack's neck. "I wish you weren't leaving tomorrow."

"I'm going to ask my boss for a few days off. We need to spend some normal time together. You know, act like tourists. Go to the beach. Dig clams. Shuck oysters. Annoy the locals. All that good stuff. What do you say?"

"It sounds very dull—and very nice. For fun, we could return to the scene of the crime."

"What do you mean?"

"A picnic at the Montauk Steps and a steam bath in the caves."

Zack said, "I look forward to getting to know you."

Lilli hugged Zack. "That sounds good to me."